Also by Rachael Reed

Sis
Sis 2 Blood on the Streets

Standalone
Codefendant
Codefendant
Once a Cheater
Once a Cheater
Passport Bro
What Happens in Prison
Preference
Sprinkle Sprinkle
Championship Bad
Street Exodus
Street Exodus
Street Royalty
Pawns of Power
SIS
Cartel Bloodline
Get Money Girls
Skip the Games
Til Death Do Us Part

Backpage Hustle
Link in Bio
The Virgin and The Kingpin
A Gangsta's Heart
Boosters
Can't Turn a Hoe Into a Housewife
Better you Than Me
Wig Dealer: How to Start Your wig Business
Trail Ride Blues
Demure Diva
Queen of the Carnival

Queen
of the
Carnival

Chapter 1: The Queen's Reign

The sweltering Caribbean sun beats down on the crowded streets of Port Antonio, the heart of Carnival in Jamaica. The air is thick with the scent of jerk chicken, marijuana, and sweat, as the rhythmic pulse of soca music vibrates through the city. Brightly colored banners and flags decorate the buildings, and the streets are a sea of vibrant costumes and gyrating bodies, all moving to the infectious beat.

In the midst of this chaos, Shakira strides down the street like a queen, her presence commanding attention. Shakira's skin glows like burnished mahogany, her curves accentuated by a tight, jeweled bodysuit that glitters in the sunlight. Shakira's long, black hair flows behind her like a mane, and her eyes are hidden behind oversized sunglasses, giving her an air of mystery. The crowd parts for Shakira as she walks, some people cheering, others whispering in awe, or fear.

Shakira is more than just a pretty face—Shakira is the undisputed Carnival Queen. Everyone knows her name, and everyone knows not to cross her. Shakira's beauty is matched only by her cunning, and she's built an empire on the backs of those foolish enough to underestimate her. The streets of Port Antonio are Shakira's domain, and the Carnival is her playground.

Shakira approaches a makeshift stage where a group of men is gathered. These men are no ordinary spectators—they are the city's elite, the ones who pull the strings behind the scenes. Among them is Councillor Davis, a slick politician with a roving eye and a greedy hand, and Mr. Chang, a wealthy businessman who controls the import and export trade. These men might have power, but they know better than to disrespect Shakira.

Councillor Davis grins as Shakira approaches. "Shakira, you lookin' like a whole snack today," Davis says, his voice dripping with lust. Shakira smirks, knowing how to play the game.

"Councillor, you always got sweet words fa mi," Shakira replies, her voice smooth as honey. Shakira knows that Davis is a dog, but Shakira also knows that he's useful. Shakira leans in close, letting him catch a whiff of her expensive perfume. "You got what I need?"

Davis nods, pulling a small envelope from his pocket and slipping it into Shakira's hand. "All set, Carnival Queen. The usual arrangements."

Shakira pockets the envelope without looking at it. "Good. You keep dis up, and mi might just let you take mi out sometime."

Davis's grin widens, and Shakira can see the hunger in his eyes. "You know I'm always ready, Shakira."

Shakira turns her attention to Mr. Chang, who watches the exchange with a shrewd eye. "And you, Mr. Chang? How's business?"

Mr. Chang gives a small nod of respect. "Business is good, thanks to your help, Shakira. The shipments have been arriving on time, no issues."

Shakira nods, satisfied. Mr. Chang handles the logistics for some of Shakira's more lucrative ventures, and so far, he hasn't let her down. "Glad to hear it. Keep it that way, and we'll all get rich."

As Shakira steps onto the stage, the crowd erupts into cheers. Shakira raises her hands, soaking in the adoration. "Port Antonio, yuh ready fi di best Carnival eva?" Shakira shouts into the microphone. The crowd roars back, and Shakira can feel the energy buzzing in the air.

Tasha, Shakira's right-hand woman, stands nearby, her eyes scanning the crowd. Tasha is a fierce, no-nonsense woman, and she's been with Shakira since day one. Tasha is the one who handles the dirty work, making sure everything runs smoothly while keeping Shakira's hands clean. Tasha knows the Carnival inside and out, and Tasha's always two steps ahead of any potential threat.

Tasha steps up beside Shakira, speaking quietly into her ear. "We got eyes on di whole place, Shakira. Everyt'ing under control."

Shakira nods, satisfied. "Good. Let's make sure dis Carnival go down in history."

As the parade kicks off, Shakira leads the way, her body moving in perfect sync with the music. Shakira dances like she's possessed, every move precise and powerful, a display of dominance that leaves no doubt who's in charge. The men in the crowd can't take their eyes off her, and Shakira knows it. Shakira uses her beauty as a weapon, and she's mastered the art of seduction. Every glance, every smile, every touch is calculated, a way to get what she wants.

As the day turns into night, the Carnival reaches its peak. The streets are packed with revelers, the music louder, the air thick with the scent of rum and weed. Shakira and Tasha make their way through the crowd, checking in with their network of contacts. The Carnival is more than just a party for Shakira—it's an opportunity to make money, close deals, and solidify her power.

At one point, Shakira and Tasha slip into a back alley, where a group of men are waiting. These men are part of Shakira's underworld network, the ones who handle the less savory aspects of her empire. Shakira's eyes narrow as she approaches them.

"Y'all got the packages ready?" Shakira asks, her tone all business.

One of the men, a wiry guy named Slim, nods. "Yeah, Shakira. Everyt'ing set. We got dem t'ings in place, jus' like yuh say."

Shakira gives a sharp nod. "Good. Make sure y'all handle di drops proper. No fuck-ups, ya hear?"

Slim and the others nod quickly, knowing better than to cross Shakira. Shakira's reputation for handling problems is well-known, and no one wants to be on the receiving end of her wrath.

As Shakira and Tasha head back to the main event, Tasha glances at Shakira. "Yuh know dey all scared of yuh, right?"

Shakira smirks, her eyes cold. "Good. Das how it supposed to be."

As the night wears on, Shakira takes a moment to survey the scene. The Carnival is in full swing, the streets alive with music, dance, and the frenetic energy of the revelers. Shakira should feel on top of the world, but there's a nagging feeling in the back of Shakira's mind, a sense that something is about to happen. Shakira pushes the feeling aside, determined to enjoy the night.

But as Shakira looks out over the crowd, she spots a figure in the distance, someone unfamiliar, someone watching her. Shakira narrows her eyes, trying to get a better look, but the figure disappears into the crowd. Shakira's gut tells her that this person is important, that they're going to play a role in whatever comes next.

Tasha notices Shakira's distraction. "Som'ting wrong?"

Shakira shakes her head, forcing a smile. "Nah, just a feelin'. Let's keep dis party goin.'"

But deep down, Shakira knows that this Carnival will be different from the others. Shakira's reign as the Carnival Queen might be at its peak, but Shakira can sense that something is looming. Something's coming and she wasn't sure what that was.

As the night goes on, Shakira continues to dance, continues to charm, continues to play the role that everyone expects of her. But the feeling of unease lingers, growing stronger with each passing moment.

Chapter 2: The Allure of Marcus

The night air in Port Antonio is thick with anticipation as Carnival reaches its max. The streets are alive with vibrant colors, pounding music, and the electric energy of people letting loose, their inhibitions tossed aside like confetti. In this world, where decadence and danger dance hand in hand, Shakira reigns supreme. But tonight, the Queen's eyes are drawn to something new, something different.

Marcus.

Marcus stands out in the crowd like a panther among house cats. Tall, dark, and dripping with confidence, Marcus navigates the streets with an air of mystery that wraps around him like a cloak. Marcus's expensive attire—sleek black slacks, a fitted shirt that clings to his muscular frame, and a Rolex that catches the light with every movement—signals wealth and power. Marcus doesn't just blend into the scene; Marcus commands it.

Shakira watches from her VIP perch, a rooftop overlooking the main parade route. The crowd below is a sea of gyrating bodies, but Shakira's gaze zeroes in on Marcus. Shakira is used to men trying to catch Shakira's attention, trying to win favor with the Carnival Queen, but Marcus doesn't even look up. Marcus moves with a purpose, as if the chaotic celebration is merely a backdrop to whatever mission Marcus is on.

"Tasha," Shakira calls out, her voice laced with curiosity and a hint of something else—something darker.

Tasha, ever observant and always by Shakira's side, steps up. "Yeah, Shakira?"

Shakira doesn't take her eyes off Marcus. "Yuh see dat man down dere? Him new. I want to know who him be."

Tasha follows Shakira's line of sight, narrowing her eyes as she assesses Marcus. "Ain't seen him before. But I'll find out."

Shakira nods, a sly smile playing on her lips. "Good. But for now, let's go introduce ourselves."

With the ease of someone born to command, Shakira descends from her perch, Tasha at her heels. Shakira weaves through the crowd, her presence parting the throng of revelers like a knife through butter. Everyone knows who Shakira is, and everyone knows better than to get in Shakira's way.

As Shakira approaches Marcus, Marcus finally looks up, their eyes locking in an instant that seems to stretch on forever. Marcus's gaze is intense, almost predatory, and Shakira feels a thrill of excitement ripple through Shakira's body. This man is dangerous, Shakira can tell, but that only makes Shakira want to know Marcus more.

"Enjoying di Carnival?" Shakira asks, her voice smooth as velvet, with just the right amount of intrigue.

Marcus smiles, a slow, deliberate curve of Marcus's lips that sends a jolt of heat through Shakira's veins. "More now that I've seen the Queen herself," Marcus replies, his voice deep and resonant, carrying a hint of a foreign accent that only adds to his allure.

Shakira raises an eyebrow, intrigued. "Yuh know who mi is, huh?"

"Hard not to," Marcus says, his eyes never leaving Shakira's. "Everyone's talkin' 'bout the Carnival Queen."

Shakira steps closer, close enough to catch the scent of Marcus's cologne—expensive, heady, intoxicating. "But yuh, mi never seen before. Yuh new to mi island?"

Marcus nods, a hint of a smirk playing on Marcus's lips. "Just arrived. Thought I'd see what all the fuss is about."

Shakira's smile widens. "Welcome, den. But be careful. Dis island can be tricky for newcomers."

Marcus chuckles, a low, rumbling sound that sends shivers down Shakira's spine. "I can handle myself, Queen."

Shakira likes Marcus's confidence, the way Marcus doesn't seem intimidated by her status. "Mi like yuh style, Marcus," Shakira says, deliberately using Marcus's name, which she knows without having to ask. Information travels fast in Shakira's world, and by the time she reached Marcus, Shakira's people had already fed Shakira what little they could find on Marcus.

"Yuh should come to mi party tonight," Shakira adds, testing Marcus's reaction. "It's where di real fun happens."

Marcus's eyes flash with interest. "Wouldn't miss it."

Satisfied, Shakira turns to leave, but not before giving Marcus a lingering look over her shoulder. "See yuh later, Marcus."

Marcus watches Shakira go, and for the first time in a long time, Shakira feels the heat of someone's gaze on her back, a gaze that makes her feel both powerful and vulnerable at the same time.

Later that night, Shakira's private party is in full swing, the music loud, the drinks flowing, and the atmosphere thick with desire. Shakira's estate, a sprawling mansion on the outskirts of the city, is a playground for the rich and dangerous. Security is tight, but Shakira knows who is coming and going—except for Marcus, who arrived as smoothly as he had caught her attention earlier.

Marcus fits right in, mingling with the elite, but Shakira notices that Marcus's eyes are always on her, no matter where Marcus is in the room. It's both thrilling and unnerving, and Shakira finds herself drawn to Marcus's side more and more as the night wears on.

"Yuh enjoying mi party?" Shakira asks as Shakira finally joins Marcus in a secluded corner of the expansive patio, away from prying eyes.

"Best part of the Carnival so far," Marcus replies, handing Shakira a glass of champagne that he seems to have conjured out of thin air.

Shakira accepts the drink, their fingers brushing as Shakira takes it, a spark of electricity passing between them. "Yuh got good taste," Shakira says, sipping the champagne and keeping her eyes on Marcus.

"Just know quality when I see it," Marcus responds, his voice low, his gaze intense.

The air between them crackles with unspoken tension, a mix of lust and something more dangerous. Shakira has played this game a thousand times before, seducing and being seduced, but this feels different. This feels like a game where the stakes are higher, where the consequences could be more than she's prepared to handle.

As the night deepens, so does their connection. Marcus and Shakira dance together, the heat of their bodies pressing close, the world around them fading away. Shakira loses track of time, lost in Marcus's touch, in Marcus's whispered words, in the way Marcus makes her feel both powerful and powerless at the same time.

By the time the party winds down, Shakira knows Marcus will not be leaving alone. Shakira takes Marcus by the hand, leading him through the winding halls of her mansion, to the master suite that overlooks the ocean. It's here, under the cover of darkness, that Shakira and Marcus finally give in to the tension that has been building all night.

Their passion is intense, explosive, leaving Shakira breathless and wanting more. But as the dawn breaks and Shakira lies in Marcus's arms, a nagging sense of unease begins to creep in. Shakira has never let anyone get this close, never let anyone distract her from her empire, from the business that keeps her on top.

But with Marcus, it's different. Shakira feels herself slipping, her priorities shifting, and it scares her. Shakira knows the dangers of letting her guard down, but Marcus's pull is too strong, too intoxicating.

As the days turn into nights and the Carnival continues, Shakira finds herself spending more and more time with Marcus, neglecting her usual duties. Meetings are missed, deals are delayed, and Tasha begins to notice the cracks forming in Shakira's carefully constructed world.

"Shakira, yuh need to focus," Tasha warns one night, after finding Shakira in Marcus's arms instead of at an important meeting. "Dis man, he's distractin' yuh. Yuh gonna lose control if yuh not careful."

But Shakira brushes Tasha off, the thrill of her new romance blinding her to the truth. "Mi got dis, Tasha. Marcus is just a fling. He don't mean nothin.'"

But deep down, Shakira knows it's a lie. Marcus means everything, and that's the problem. Shakira is caught in a web of desire and deception, and Shakira's no longer sure if she's the one in control.

The allure of Marcus is strong, but Shakira can't shake the feeling that she's playing with fire, and that sooner or later, she's going to get burned.

Chapter 3: A Shift in Power

The humid air hangs heavy over Port Antonio, the sun sinking low and casting long shadows across the streets. The Carnival may be in full swing, but there's a different kind of tension simmering beneath the surface—a tension that has nothing to do with the festivities and everything to do with the shifting power dynamics in Shakira's world.

Shakira is at her estate, draped across a plush chaise in her opulent living room, a glass of wine in hand. The room is bathed in the warm glow of candlelight, casting flickering shadows on the walls. It should be a scene of luxury and power, but there's an undercurrent of unease that Shakira can't quite shake.

Marcus is in the next room, handling a phone call that Shakira wasn't privy to, and Shakira doesn't like that. Shakira prides herself on being in control of every situation, but ever since Marcus came into Shakira's life, things have been slipping through Shakira's fingers. Marcus has a way of making Shakira feel both powerful and powerless, and it's starting to mess with her head.

Tasha, ever the observant one, watches from across the room, her expression unreadable. Tasha's been with Shakira for years—through the rise, the blood, the hustle—and Tasha knows Shakira better than anyone. And what Tasha sees now has her worried.

"Shakira," Tasha says, breaking the silence, "we need to talk."

Shakira glances up, arching an eyebrow. "'Bout what?"

Tasha steps closer, her voice low and serious. "'Bout him," Tasha says, jerking her chin toward the room where Marcus is still on the phone. "Dis man... yuh don't know him like dat. And he's got yuh actin' different."

Shakira waves a hand dismissively, not wanting to hear it. "Tasha, yuh always worry too much. Marcus ain't no threat. Him jus' new. Him don't know how we do t'ings yet."

Tasha frowns, her concern deepening. "Nah, Shakira. It ain't jus' dat. Yuh ain't been yaself since him come 'round. Yuh missin' meetings, yuh leavin' t'ings undone... dis ain't like yuh."

Shakira bristles, setting her glass down with a little more force than necessary. "I'm still runnin' t'ings, Tasha. Ain't nobody takin' my place. Marcus jus'... got my attention right now, dat's all."

Tasha narrows her eyes, not convinced. "Yuh sure it ain't more dan dat? Yuh sure he ain't tryin' to play yuh?"

Shakira scoffs, leaning back and crossing her legs. "Please. Yuh really t'ink mi lettin' some man play mi? I got dis, Tasha. I know what I'm doin.'"

But Tasha doesn't let it go. "Yuh remember di last time yuh let someone close, Shakira? Look what happen den."

The reminder stings, but Shakira doesn't let it show. Shakira's learned from those mistakes—Shakira's not the same woman she was back then. "Dat was different," Shakira says, her tone sharp. "Dis is different."

Before Tasha can respond, Marcus reappears, phone call over. Marcus's presence immediately shifts the energy in the room, his easy smile and confident stride commanding attention. "Everything cool?" Marcus asks, sliding into the seat next to Shakira like Marcus belongs there.

Shakira forces a smile, ignoring the tension between herself and Tasha. "Yeah, everything cool."

But the look Marcus gives Tasha—calculated, assessing—doesn't go unnoticed. Marcus knows that Tasha is the gatekeeper, the one who has Shakira's ear. If Marcus is going to get what Marcus wants, Tasha has to be dealt with, one way or another.

The next few days are a blur of Carnival events and late-night rendezvous. Marcus is always by Shakira's side, a shadow that's both comforting and disconcerting. Marcus attends meetings with Shakira, meets her contacts, starts to learn the ins and outs of her operation.

And slowly, without Shakira even realizing it, Marcus starts to edge in on Shakira's territory.

It starts small—a suggestion here, a bit of advice there—but soon it seems Marcus is taking on more responsibilities, making decisions that should be Shakira's to make. And Shakira, caught up in the whirlwind of their affair, lets it happen. Marcus's influence is intoxicating, and Shakira finds herself relying on Marcus more and more, even though Tasha's warnings still echo in the back of her mind.

One night, after another lavish party, Tasha pulls Shakira aside, frustration etched into Tasha's features. "Shakira, dis ain't right," Tasha says, her voice low but urgent. "Marcus ain't who he say him is. Him too comfortable, too quick. Yuh need to open yuh eyes."

Shakira is tired, worn out from the relentless pace of the Carnival and the emotional tug-of-war that's been brewing inside Shakira. Shakira's patience snaps. "Tasha, enough! Mi tell yuh, mi got dis! Stop treatin' mi like some fool who don't know what's what!"

Tasha holds her ground, her eyes hard. "Den act like yuh got dis, Shakira. Act like di queen yuh is, not some girl who lose herself over a man."

The words hit their mark, and for a moment, Shakira falters. But Marcus appears again, wrapping an arm around Shakira's waist, pulling her close. Marcus whispers something in Shakira's ear—something that makes Shakira smile, and just like that, the moment is gone. Shakira shrugs off Tasha's concerns, choosing instead to lean into the warmth of Marcus's embrace.

But behind that smile, the unease is growing. Shakira can feel it in the pit of Shakira's stomach, a gnawing doubt that refuses to be silenced. And as Shakira watches Marcus charm and manipulate his way through her world, that doubt begins to take root, threatening to unravel everything Shakira has built.

Meanwhile, Marcus's true intentions are beginning to surface. Marcus's phone calls—always taken in private—are to people Shakira doesn't know, about things Marcus doesn't explain. Marcus's questions about Shakira's operations are too specific, too probing. And then there's the way Marcus interacts with Shakira's contacts—like Marcus is sizing them up, weighing their worth.

One afternoon, while Shakira is out handling a meeting, Marcus makes a call that changes everything. Marcus's voice, usually smooth and charming, is cold and calculating as Marcus speaks into the phone. "Yeah, she's hooked. Ain't gonna take much longer. Once we got the network, we move in. She won't know what hit her."

The conversation is quick, precise, and when Marcus hangs up, there's a satisfied gleam in Marcus's eyes. Marcus knows that Shakira's empire is ripe for the taking, and all Marcus needs to do is keep playing the role, keep feeding into Shakira's desires, until the time is right to strike.

By the time Shakira returns, Marcus is back to being the attentive lover, all smiles and sweet words. And Shakira, caught up in the game they're playing, misses the signs—the way Marcus's eyes dart away when Shakira asks a question, the slight tension in Marcus's jaw when Shakira mentions Tasha's concerns.

Shakira is standing on the balcony of her estate, looking out over the city that she's ruled for so long. But something is different now. The lights seem dimmer, the streets quieter. The power that once surged through her veins feels distant, like it's slipping away.

Shakira's grip on her empire is loosening, and Shakira can feel it. But instead of confronting the truth, Shakira buries the doubt, telling herself that she's still in control, that Marcus is just a distraction, nothing more.

But deep down, Shakira knows that this is a lie. Marcus is more than a distraction. Marcus is a threat, one that Shakira is not prepared for.

The shift in power has begun, and Shakira is caught in the middle of it, too blinded by desire and denial to see the danger that's closing in.

Chapter 4: The Party Before the Fall

The night air is thick with humidity, the kind that clings to the skin and makes everything feel a little more intense. In the hills above Port Antonio, Shakira's estate glows like a beacon of wealth and power, its sprawling grounds lit up with the soft golden glow of hundreds of lanterns. The sound of laughter and music floats through the air, mingling with the scent of expensive cigars, rum, and tropical flowers.

It's Carnival season, and this is the night everyone's been waiting for—Shakira's annual Carnival party, an event that has become legendary on the island. The who's who of Port Antonio's elite are in attendance: politicians, businessmen, entertainers, and those who run the city's underworld from the shadows. It's a night for power plays and whispered deals, for flaunting wealth and status, and Shakira is at the center of it all, the undisputed Carnival Queen.

Shakira stands at the top of a grand staircase, overlooking the scene below. Shakira's dressed in a gown that clings to every curve, shimmering with a thousand tiny sequins that catch the light as Shakira moves. Shakira's hair is piled high in an elaborate updo, adorned with jewels that sparkle like stars. To anyone looking at Shakira, it seems like Shakira has it all—beauty, power, control.

But as Shakira descends the staircase, Marcus at Shakira's side, there's an undercurrent of tension in the air that Shakira can't quite ignore. The guests greet Shakira with smiles and compliments, but Shakira notices the way their eyes flicker to Marcus, the way their smiles falter for just a fraction of a second before they recover.

Marcus, as always, is the picture of charm and confidence. Marcus moves through the crowd with ease, a glass of champagne in hand, flashing that winning smile that Shakira has come to know so well. But tonight, there's something different in the way Marcus carries himself—something almost predatory.

Tasha is there too, hovering at the edge of the crowd like a shadow. Tasha's eyes never leave Marcus, and every time Tasha catches Shakira's gaze, there's a warning there, unspoken but loud and clear. Shakira has always trusted Tasha's instincts, but tonight, Shakira is determined to push those doubts aside. Tonight is about celebrating Shakira's reign, showing the world that Shakira is still in control.

As the night wears on, the party becomes more extravagant. The music pulses through the air, a mix of soca, dancehall, and reggaeton that makes the ground vibrate. The guests dance, drink, and laugh, but underneath it all, there's a sense of something looming, like a storm that hasn't yet broken.

Shakira and Marcus are the center of attention, and Shakira plays the role to perfection. Shakira dances with Marcus, their bodies moving in perfect sync, the heat between them palpable. The guests watch with a mix of admiration and envy, but Shakira can sense the whispers that ripple through the crowd.

"Who is this man?"

"Where did he come from?"

"He's got her wrapped around his finger."

Shakira hears the murmurs, but Shakira forces a smile, leaning into Marcus as they move across the dance floor. Shakira can't afford to show any weakness, not now, not when everyone is watching.

But as the night progresses, the whispers grow louder, and Shakira can feel the unease building inside Shakira. It's in the way the guests' gazes linger on Marcus, in the way Tasha's eyes narrow every time Marcus speaks to someone new. It's in the way Shakira's closest allies seem distant, their usual warmth replaced with a guardedness that Shakira can't quite put her finger on. Shakira brushes it off as paranoia, chalking it up to the stress of maintaining her empire during the most intense season of the year. But deep down, Shakira knows something is off.

As the party reaches its peak, Shakira leads Marcus out to the terrace overlooking the ocean. The view is breathtaking—the moonlight dancing on the waves, the sound of the distant surf mingling with the music from inside. But even here, away from the prying eyes of the guests, Shakira can't shake the feeling that something is wrong.

Marcus pulls Shakira close, his hand resting on the small of her back. "You're quiet tonight, Queen," Marcus murmurs, his voice low and smooth, laced with that accent Shakira has come to find so irresistible. "Everything alright?"

Shakira forces a smile, but it doesn't reach her eyes. "Just tired, is all. Carnival's always a lot of work."

Marcus tilts his head, studying Shakira with those dark, unreadable eyes. "You're the Queen. You're supposed to enjoy it."

Shakira laughs, but it sounds hollow even to her. "Enjoyment comes later. Tonight, it's about keeping everything in check."

Marcus leans in, his lips brushing against Shakira's ear as he whispers, "You don't always have to be in control, you know."

The words send a shiver down Shakira's spine, but they also ignite something in her—something that's been simmering since the night Marcus walked into her life. The need to let go, to relinquish control, if only for a moment. But the very thought of it terrifies Shakira.

"Control is what keeps me on top," Shakira replies, her voice firmer now. "It's what keeps people in line."

Marcus pulls back slightly, a knowing smile playing on his lips. "And here I thought you trusted me."

Shakira's eyes narrow, searching Marcus's face for any sign of duplicity, but all Shakira sees is confidence, the same confidence that has both drawn her in and kept her on edge since the beginning. "I trust you," Shakira says slowly, though the words feel heavy in her mouth.

"Good," Marcus says, pressing a kiss to Shakira's forehead. "Because I'm here for you, Queen. Always."

But as Marcus's lips linger on Shakira's skin, the unease inside her swells. It's not just the party, not just the whispers—it's something more, something Shakira can't quite name. Shakira knows Marcus is hiding something, but she's not sure what, and that uncertainty gnaws at her.

Just as Shakira is about to pull away, Tasha steps onto the terrace, her expression grim. "Shakira, we need to talk."

Marcus's eyes flick to Tasha, a brief flash of irritation crossing his features before he masks it with a charming smile. "Can't it wait, Tasha? We were just—"

"No, it can't," Tasha interrupts, her tone leaving no room for argument.

Shakira sighs, extricating herself from Marcus's embrace. "Go inside, Marcus. I'll be in soon."

Marcus hesitates for a moment, his gaze flicking between Tasha and Shakira, but eventually, he nods and heads back into the house. Once he's gone, Tasha steps closer, her voice low but urgent. "Shakira, dis man... he ain't what he seems."

Shakira rolls her eyes, frustration bubbling up. "Tasha, not dis again. I already told yuh—"

"No, Shakira, yuh listen dis time," Tasha snaps, her eyes blazing. "I been hearin' tings. Real tings. Marcus is makin' moves behind yuh back. Talkin' to people he shouldn't be talkin' to. Yuh gotta be careful."

Shakira's heart skips a beat, but she forces herself to stay calm. "What kinda moves?"

"Settin' up meetings with some of di old guard," Tasha says, her voice tight. "And not di friendly kind. Di kinda meetings where alliances shift, where power changes hands."

Shakira's blood runs cold. "Yuh sure 'bout dis, Tasha?"

"Wouldn't be tellin' yuh if I wasn't," Tasha replies. "Yuh need to open yuh eyes, Shakira. Yuh need to see what's really goin' on."

For a moment, Shakira feels the world tilt beneath her feet, the weight of Tasha's words crashing down on her. But then Shakira shakes her head, refusing to believe it. "Marcus wouldn't do dat. Him got no reason to."

Tasha narrows her eyes. "Maybe yuh blinded by him charm, Shakira, but I'm tellin' yuh—he's usin' yuh. And if yuh don't do somethin' 'bout it, it's gonna be too late."

Shakira's mind races, a storm of doubt and fear swirling inside her. But even as the uncertainty gnaws at her, there's a part of Shakira that refuses to let go of the image Shakira has built of Marcus—the man who swept her off her feet, who made her feel alive in a way she hadn't in years.

"Tasha, yuh need to trust mi," Shakira says, though the conviction in her voice is shaky. "I know what I'm doin'."

Tasha's eyes harden, but she nods. "I hope yuh right, Shakira. For yuh sake."

As Tasha walks back inside, leaving Shakira alone on the terrace, the weight of the night settles on Shakira's shoulders. The laughter and music from the party feel distant, muffled by the doubt that has taken root in Shakira's mind. Shakira knows Tasha wouldn't lie, but the idea of Marcus betraying her... it's too much to accept. Not yet.

But as Shakira looks out over the glittering lights of her estate, the truth begins to seep in, cold and undeniable. The empire she has built, the power she has fought so hard to maintain—it's all more fragile than Shakira ever realized. And Marcus... Marcus might just be the one to bring it all crashing down.

Chapter 5: The Betrayal

The air in Port Antonio is thick with the excitement of Carnival, the biggest celebration of the year. The streets are alive with the sound of soca music, the vibrant colors of costumes, and the energy of a people reveling in their freedom. But for Shakira, the Carnival Queen, this night will mark the beginning of her downfall.

Shakira's estate is the epicenter of the night's festivities. The sprawling mansion, perched on a hill overlooking the city, is decked out in lights, the driveway lined with luxury cars as the island's elite arrive for the most anticipated party of the season. Inside, the music is loud, the drinks are flowing, and the atmosphere is electric. Everyone who's anyone is there, and all eyes are on Shakira, who moves through the crowd like a goddess, her presence commanding respect and admiration.

Shakira is dressed to kill in a dazzling gold dress that clings to her every curve, her hair flowing in waves down her back, a crown of jewels atop her head. Shakira's arm is linked with Marcus's, who looks every bit the part of the powerful man at her side, his tailored suit sharp and his smile charming. They make a striking couple, the center of attention, and as they move through the crowd, Shakira can feel the eyes of her guests on them—some envious, some admiring, and a few, like Tasha, wary.

Tasha watches from the edge of the room, her eyes never leaving Marcus. Tasha's been uneasy about him for weeks, and tonight, something feels off. There's a tension in the air, a sense that something isn't right, but Tasha can't quite put her finger on it. Tasha's instincts, honed from years of living and surviving in the streets, are screaming at her, but Shakira won't listen. Shakira is too caught up in the whirlwind that is Marcus, too blinded by desire and trust to see the danger lurking in the shadows.

As the night wears on, the party reaches its peak. The music gets louder, the drinks stronger, and the guests more uninhibited. Shakira basks in the glow of it all, feeling on top of the world. Shakira's empire is at its zenith, her power unquestioned, her influence unmatched. But beneath the surface, the cracks are beginning to show.

In a darkened corner of the mansion, Marcus slips away to make a call. His voice is low, his tone cold, as he speaks into the phone. "It's time. Everything's in place. Make sure it's clean—no loose ends." Marcus hangs up, slipping the phone back into his pocket, his expression unreadable. Marcus's plan is in motion, and there's no turning back now.

Meanwhile, Shakira is on the dance floor, surrounded by admirers, her body moving to the rhythm of the music. Shakira feels alive, electric, unaware that the walls are closing in around her. Marcus returns, sliding an arm around Shakira's waist, pulling her close. "You're the queen of the night, Shakira," Marcus whispers in her ear, his breath hot against her skin. Shakira smiles, leaning into Marcus, feeling invincible.

But outside, the mood is shifting. Unmarked cars pull up to the estate, men in plain clothes stepping out, their faces grim. The police have arrived, and they're not here to join the party.

Inside, Tasha feels the shift, her eyes narrowing as she senses the change in the air. Tasha looks around, noticing the subtle movements—guests whispering, glances exchanged, the sudden tension that grips the room. Tasha's heart races, dread curling in her stomach. Something is about to go down, and Tasha knows it's bad.

Suddenly, the doors burst open, and the police flood the room, their presence commanding immediate attention. The music stops, and the partygoers freeze, a collective gasp rippling through the crowd. The lead officer steps forward, his eyes locked on Shakira. "Shakira Williams, you're under arrest for drug trafficking and conspiracy."

Shakira's world tilts, the words not making sense at first. Shakira looks at Marcus, confusion and shock written across her face, but Marcus's expression is stony, unreadable. Shakira's mind races, trying to make sense of what's happening, but there's no time. The officers move in, grabbing Shakira's arms, pulling her away from Marcus, slapping cuffs on her wrists.

The room erupts into chaos. Guests scramble to get out, some pulling out their phones, capturing the scene as Shakira, the Carnival Queen, is led away in handcuffs. The officers are rough, not caring that Shakira is in a delicate dress, not caring that she's the host of this lavish party. Shakira struggles, trying to maintain her composure, but the fear is creeping in, the realization that this is real, that she's been set up.

Tasha pushes through the crowd, trying to reach Shakira, but the officers block Tasha's path. "Let her go!" Tasha shouts, but they don't listen. Tasha turns to Marcus, fury in Tasha's eyes. "What did yuh do?!"

But Marcus just stands there, watching as Shakira is taken away. Marcus's face is a mask of indifference, but there's a cold satisfaction in Marcus's eyes. Marcus played his part perfectly, and now Shakira is the one paying the price.

As Shakira is dragged outside, the cameras flash, reporters shouting questions, the lights blinding. The Carnival that was supposed to be the height of her reign has become the scene of her downfall. Shakira feels exposed, vulnerable, the power she once wielded slipping away with every step.

The police shove Shakira into the back of a cruiser, slamming the door shut. Shakira's heart pounds in Shakira's chest, panic setting in. Shakira's mind races, trying to figure out what went wrong, how Marcus could betray her like this. Shakira trusted Marcus, let Marcus into her world, and now everything is crumbling around her.

Back inside the mansion, the party is over. The guests are gone, the music silenced, and the once-vibrant atmosphere replaced with an eerie quiet. Marcus stands alone in the empty room, a glass of whiskey in Marcus's hand. Marcus swirls the liquid, watching the amber liquid catch the light, a small smile playing on Marcus's lips.

Marcus's phone buzzes, and Marcus answers, listening as the voice on the other end confirms what Marcus already knows. "It's done. She's out of the way."

Marcus nods, ending the call. Marcus played Shakira like a fiddle, using her trust, her desire, her power, and now Marcus has it all. Shakira's empire is his for the taking, and there's no one left to stand in Marcus's way.

As the cruiser pulls away, Shakira watches the lights of her mansion fade into the distance, tears stinging her eyes. Shakira's world has been turned upside down, and Shakira knows there's no going back. Everything Shakira worked for, everything Shakira built, is gone.

Chapter 6: Public Humiliation

The cold metal bars of the cell press into Shakira's back as she sits on the hard, unforgiving bench. The fluorescent lights buzz overhead, casting a harsh glow on the grimy concrete floor. Shakira's head is spinning, the events of the past twenty-four hours playing in a relentless loop in her mind. The betrayal, the arrest, the loss—everything Shakira built has crumbled in an instant, leaving Shakira reeling in disbelief.

Outside, the world has turned on Shakira. The media, which once glorified Shakira as the dazzling Carnival Queen, now paints Shakira as the face of corruption and crime. Every news outlet is plastered with Shakira's mugshot, taken just hours after Shakira was dragged out of her own party in handcuffs. The same media that once celebrated Shakira's every move now tears Shakira down, their headlines dripping with venom.

"Carnival Queen or Crime Boss? The Downfall of Shakira Williams."

"From Glitter to Grit: Shakira Williams Exposed as Drug Lord."

"Shakira Williams: The Dark Side of the Carnival Queen."

The stories are sensationalized, the facts twisted and distorted to fit the narrative that Shakira was never a queen but a villain hiding in plain sight. They dig up every piece of dirt they can find on Shakira, embellishing rumors and gossip until they become damning evidence of Shakira's supposed criminal empire.

As Shakira sits in that cold, lonely cell, Shakira can hear the jeers and taunts from the other prisoners, their voices echoing off the walls. "Look at di mighty queen now!" one shouts, laughter following the taunt. "Big bad Carnival Queen, huh? Where's yuh crown now?"

Shakira's heart pounds in Shakira's chest, a mixture of rage and humiliation burning in Shakira's veins. Shakira was once on top, the one everyone feared and respected. Now, Shakira's just another prisoner, stripped of her power, her dignity, her identity.

But the worst part isn't the media or the taunts—it's the silence from those Shakira once called friends. The people who swore loyalty to Shakira, who profited from Shakira's success, have all gone silent. No visits, no messages, no one coming to her defense. Even Tasha, Shakira's closest confidante, the one who was always by Shakira's side, is nowhere to be found.

Shakira's first night in jail is a nightmare. The bed is a thin mattress on a metal frame, the sheets rough and itchy. The sounds of the jail—the clanging of doors, the shouts of the guards, the cries of the other inmates—keep Shakira on edge, unable to sleep. Every time Shakira closes her eyes, Shakira sees Marcus's face, his cold, calculating eyes staring back at her, the realization of his betrayal hitting Shakira all over again.

By morning, Shakira's mind is made up. Shakira needs to get out of here, needs to find a way to clear her name and take back what's hers. But as the day drags on and the reality of her situation sinks in, Shakira realizes that it won't be that easy. Shakira's lawyer, who barely glances at Shakira during their meeting, tells Shakira that the charges are serious and the evidence against Shakira is overwhelming. The drugs they found at Shakira's party, the money laundering, the informant testimonies—it all points to Shakira being guilty.

"Yuh lookin' at some serious time," the lawyer says, his voice flat, emotionless. "They got yuh dead to rights."

Shakira can hardly believe what she's hearing. Shakira tries to explain that it's a setup, that Marcus is the one behind it all, but the lawyer just nods, his expression one of practiced indifference. "Everyone say they innocent," the lawyer says, closing his briefcase. "Best bet is to plea. Maybe they'll cut yuh a deal."

Shakira's blood boils at the thought of pleading guilty to something without a fight, but the lawyer's words echo in her mind long after he leaves. The system is stacked against her, and without allies, without money, Shakira is facing a long, uphill battle. Shakira's used to fighting, but this is a different kind of war—one Shakira's not sure she can win.

Later that day, Shakira is escorted to a small room where she's allowed a phone call. The guard watches her closely as Shakira dials Tasha's number, her hands trembling. Shakira's heart pounds in her chest as the phone rings, each second stretching into an eternity. But Tasha doesn't answer. Shakira tries again, and again, but each time, the call goes to voicemail. The realization that Tasha is avoiding her is a punch to the gut. Shakira hangs up the phone, feeling more alone than ever.

The news spreads quickly through the streets of Port Antonio. The once-feared and revered Shakira Williams is now a pariah. Her former associates, those who once thrived under her reign, distance themselves as fast as they can, eager to avoid the fallout. Shakira's empire is crumbling, and with it, the loyalty she thought she commanded.

Even Shakira's allies in the underworld, those who benefited from her connections and power, have turned their backs on her. Shakira's calls go unanswered, her messages ignored. No one wants to be associated with a sinking ship, and right now, Shakira is sinking fast.

As the days pass, the media frenzy only intensifies. Reporters camp outside the courthouse, waiting for any scrap of information they can turn into a headline. The stories become more and more sensationalized, each one painting a darker picture of Shakira. The public, once captivated by her beauty and power, now revels in her downfall. The Carnival Queen has become the villain of the story, and there's no redemption in sight.

Shakira is moved to a different cell, this one even smaller and more isolated than the last. The walls feel like they're closing in on her, the silence deafening. Shakira spends hours staring at the ceiling, trying to figure out where it all went wrong. Shakira trusted Marcus, let him into her life, and now Shakira is paying the price. The anger and betrayal gnaw at her, but there's nothing she can do. Shakira is trapped, both physically and mentally, with no way out.

The guards aren't kind to her, either. They know who she is, or rather, who she was, and they take pleasure in her fall from grace. They taunt her, calling her the Carnival Queen in mocking tones, laughing at her expense. Shakira tries to block it out, but it's impossible. The humiliation is constant, a reminder of how far she's fallen.

One night, as Shakira lies on her cot, staring up at the cracked ceiling, she hears a noise outside her cell. Shakira sits up, her heart racing, as the door swings open and a figure steps inside. It's Tasha, looking more haggard and worn than Shakira has ever seen her.

"Tasha," Shakira says, relief flooding through her. "Where yuh been?"

Tasha doesn't meet Shakira's eyes. Instead, Tasha stands there, hands shoved into her pockets, her gaze fixed on the floor. "Shakira, mi sorry," Tasha says, her voice barely above a whisper. "But I can't help yuh no more. It's too dangerous."

Shakira's stomach drops. "What yuh mean? Yuh gonna leave mi here?"

Tasha nods, still not looking at Shakira. "Marcus got connections, Shakira. Mi can't go up against dat."

Shakira's heart breaks at the words. Tasha was the last person Shakira thought would abandon her, but here she is, doing just that. "So yuh just gonna walk away? After everything?"

Tasha finally looks up, her eyes filled with regret. "Mi don't got a choice, Shakira. Dis bigger than both of us. Yuh gotta understand. But mi got you a hearing with the lawyer to help free yuh for now."

Shakira doesn't respond, too numb to feel anything but the crushing weight of her situation. Tasha hesitates for a moment, then turns and walks out of the cell, leaving Shakira alone once more. The door slams shut, the sound echoing through the empty hallways, a final punctuation to the conversation, and to their friendship.

The betrayal stings worse than anything else. Shakira curls up on the cot, tears spilling down her cheeks as the reality of her isolation sets in. Shakira is alone, completely and utterly alone, with no one left to turn to.

Chapter 7: Stripped of Power

The iron gates that once marked the entrance to Shakira's mansion creak open, rusted and forgotten, as Shakira steps out of the cab that has brought her back to this place that no longer feels like home. The driver watches her through the rearview mirror, his eyes filled with the pity that Shakira despises. She nods at him curtly and hands him the last of her cash before turning her back on the only thing that still felt somewhat familiar—the cab, now rolling away, leaving her stranded in the remnants of a life that no longer exists.

Shakira stands at the entrance of what was once her kingdom, but the grandeur has faded. The lush gardens that used to surround her mansion are now overgrown, the flowers that once bloomed brightly now wilted and dying. The house itself looks abandoned, its windows dark, and its walls streaked with dirt. It's as if the house itself has given up, knowing its queen no longer reigns.

The once bustling driveway is empty, save for the stray leaves that the wind has gathered. Shakira's heart aches as she pushes open the front door, the hinges squealing in protest. Inside, the house is a hollow shell of what it once was. The grand chandelier that used to sparkle with opulence now hangs dim, half of its bulbs dead. The furniture, once polished and pristine, is covered in dust, as if forgotten in her absence. Shakira's footsteps echo through the empty halls, the sound amplifying the loneliness that has taken root in her chest.

Marcus has taken everything.

Shakira walks through each room, the reality of her situation crashing down with every step. The art on the walls is gone, the expensive vases and statues that used to decorate the spaces are missing. Even the custom drapes have been stripped from the windows, leaving them bare and cold. The place where she used to entertain the island's elite is now just a skeleton of memories—echoes of laughter and music that once filled these halls now replaced by an eerie silence.

Shakira stops in the living room, her eyes falling on the one thing that Marcus didn't take: a small framed photo of her and Tasha, taken during one of the first Carnivals they ruled together. Shakira's fingers tremble as she picks it up, her reflection mingling with the image of her former self—confident, powerful, untouchable. But that woman is gone, replaced by someone Shakira barely recognizes.

The phone in her pocket buzzes, startling her out of her thoughts. Shakira pulls it out, hoping—praying—it's Tasha. But it's just a news alert, another story about her downfall. Shakira's thumb hovers over the screen for a moment before she shoves the phone back into her pocket, refusing to read it. Shakira knows what they're saying—how the Carnival Queen has been dethroned, how she's become the island's newest cautionary tale, a lesson in hubris and trust gone wrong.

Shakira leaves the mansion behind, unable to bear the sight of it any longer. There's nothing left for her there. As she walks out into the harsh light of day, the sun seems to mock her, shining down on a world that no longer feels like her own.

Shakira's journey to Gullyside is a nightmare. The streets she once ruled with an iron fist now feel foreign, the people who once feared her now openly mock her. Shakira hears the whispers as she passes by—the snickers, the cruel jokes, the hushed conversations that stop the moment they realize she can hear them.

"Look at di mighty fall," one man says, loud enough for Shakira to hear. "Yuh see how she look now? Just another rat in di gutter."

Shakira keeps her head high, refusing to let them see her break. But inside, she's crumbling, every word slicing through her pride like a knife.

When she finally arrives at Gullyside, it's worse than she imagined. The building is a crumbling relic, barely standing on its foundation. The walls are cracked and peeling, the stairs leading up to her new apartment dangerously unstable. The smell of decay and neglect permeates the air, a constant reminder of where she is now—a place she never thought she'd be.

Shakira pushes open the door to her new apartment, the rusty hinges creaking in protest. The space is small, barely more than a single room with a kitchenette and a bathroom that looks like it hasn't been cleaned in years. The walls are stained, the floorboards creak with every step, and the single window is barred, letting in just enough light to make the room feel like a prison.

Shakira drops her bag on the floor, the sound echoing in the empty space. She sinks down onto the bed—a lumpy, uncomfortable mattress that sinks under her weight—and stares at the ceiling, trying to process everything that's happened.

Marcus has taken everything from her.

Her mind races with thoughts of revenge, but each plan she tries to formulate crumbles under the weight of her reality. She has no money, no allies, and no power. Marcus played her, used her, and now he's left her with nothing. And worst of all, he's taken her reputation, turning the island against her.

Shakira's name, once synonymous with power and success, is now a cautionary tale among the island's underworld. The Carnival Queen who had it all but lost it because she trusted the wrong man. The whispers grow louder with each passing day, her name dragged through the mud in every corner of the city.

Shakira knows she should fight, that she should claw her way back to the top, but the weight of her loss is suffocating. Every step feels like a struggle, every breath like a battle. The streets that once revered her now mock her, and the thought of facing them again feels unbearable.

As the days turn into nights, Shakira falls into a routine of survival. She scrounges for food, her once lavish meals now replaced by scraps and cheap takeout. She avoids the people she once knew, their faces now filled with either pity or contempt. Shakira becomes a ghost in her own city, slipping through the shadows, avoiding the light that once shone so brightly on her.

But no matter how hard she tries to fade away, the memories haunt her. The laughter, the music, the feeling of power coursing through her veins—now replaced by the crushing silence of her new reality. Shakira lies awake at night, staring at the ceiling, replaying the events over and over again, trying to find a way to undo what's been done. But there's no going back. The Carnival Queen is no more.

Chapter 8: Confronting the Betrayal

The sun hangs low in the sky, casting a dull orange glow over the streets of Port Antonio as Shakira steps out of her rundown apartment. The air is thick with the scent of the sea, mingling with the stench of sweat, fried food, and the faint undercurrent of decay that clings to the neglected parts of the city. The neighborhood is a far cry from the life Shakira once knew—no more luxury cars, no more designer clothes, no more adoring crowds. The Carnival Queen has been dethroned, and now Shakira walks the streets like a ghost, haunted by what she's lost.

Shakira pulls her jacket tighter around herself, not just against the evening chill but against the cold reality of her situation. The streets that once buzzed with whispers of her name now hold only echoes of mockery and disdain. Shakira can hear the snickers of passersby, the muttered comments, the sideways glances that cut deeper than any blade.

"Look who it is, di fallin' queen," someone sneers as Shakira passes by. Shakira's jaw tightens, but Shakira keeps walking, forcing herself to ignore it.

But it's not just the words that hurt—it's the realization that a man has stolen everything from her. Not just her wealth, not just her home, but her identity, her power. The empire that Shakira built from the ground up, the reputation Shakira carved out for herself in this unforgiving world, has been taken from her.

As Shakira makes her way through the streets, the full extent of Marcus's betrayal hits her like a sucker punch. Marcus didn't just steal her empire; Marcus erased her. The people who once bowed to Shakira, who feared and respected her, now look at Marcus with the same deference they once showed Shakira. Marcus has filled the void Shakira left behind, and he's done it so seamlessly that it's like Shakira never existed.

Shakira's mind races as Shakira walks, trying to piece together how it all went so wrong. Shakira trusted Marcus, let Marcus into her life, her bed, her heart. And Marcus used that trust to destroy her. Shakira's hands clench into fists, the rage bubbling up inside her, threatening to consume her. But along with the rage is a deep, gnawing fear—fear that Shakira is truly alone now, with no allies, no friends, no way out.

Shakira's feet carry her to a familiar spot—a small, tucked-away corner of the city where she used to meet with her closest associates, where deals were made and plans were hatched. But as Shakira approaches, Shakira feels a chill run down her spine. The place is deserted, the usual activity replaced by an eerie silence. Shakira's heart sinks as the realization sets in: no one is coming. The people who once had Shakira's back have all turned away.

Shakira leans against the wall, the rough brick scraping against her back. Shakira's breathing is heavy, each breath a struggle as the weight of her situation presses down on her. Shakira thought she was invincible, thought she could handle anything that came her way. But now, with everything stripped away, Shakira feels small, vulnerable, like a lamb in a den of wolves.

A rustling sound pulls Shakira from her thoughts, and she turns to see a figure emerging from the shadows. For a moment, hope flares in Shakira's chest—maybe it's someone who can help, someone who hasn't abandoned her. But as the figure steps into the dim light, Shakira's heart sinks once more. It's not an ally—it's a reminder of the life Shakira used to lead.

The figure is a man, one of the many low-level hustlers who once worked for Shakira. His face is familiar, but now it's twisted with a sneer of disdain. "What yuh doin' here, Shakira?" he asks, his voice dripping with contempt. "Ain't no place for yuh no more."

Shakira's mouth goes dry, but Shakira forces herself to stand tall, to meet his gaze without flinching. "I built dis place," Shakira says, her voice low and steady."

The man chuckles, shaking his head. "And look where dat got yuh. Dat man took everything yuh had, and yuh ain't got nothin' left. Best yuh move on, Shakira. Ain't nobody here for yuh no more."

The words sting, but Shakira refuses to let it show. Shakira's anger flares, pushing back the fear and despair. "I ain't goin' nowhere," Shakira says, her voice firm. "Dis still my city, my streets."

The man shrugs, unimpressed. "We'll see 'bout dat. But if I were yuh, I'd be careful."

With that, the man turns and disappears back into the shadows, leaving Shakira alone once more. Shakira's heart pounds in her chest, the reality of her situation sinking in deeper with each passing moment. Shakira's been reduced to a shadow of her former self, a cautionary tale whispered among the underworld—a reminder that even the mightiest can fall.

As Shakira makes her way back to her apartment, the weight of Marcus's betrayal presses down on her, threatening to crush her under its force. Shakira's thoughts are a chaotic whirlwind—how did it come to this? How did Shakira let Marcus get so close, so deep under her skin that Marcus could dismantle everything Shakira built?

Back in her dingy apartment, Shakira paces the small living room, her mind racing. Shakira can't stay here, can't let Marcus win. But every time Shakira thinks of a way to fight back, it feels like hitting a brick wall. Marcus has too much power now, too much influence. Shakira's resources are gone, her allies scattered, her name tarnished beyond repair.

Shakira collapses onto the threadbare couch, her head in her hands. Shakira's never felt so lost, so powerless. The streets that once bowed to Shakira now mock her, the people who once feared her now pity her. Shakira is a queen without a kingdom, a fighter without a cause.

Chapter 9: The Depths of Despair

The morning sun barely peeks over the horizon, casting a dull, gray light over Port Antonio's worn and gritty streets. Shakira steps out of her rundown apartment, the stale air of the cramped space clinging to her like a second skin. There's no room for pride now—just survival. Shakira's once-queenly gait is now a hurried shuffle, her eyes scanning the surroundings with wary vigilance. The city she once ruled is now a minefield of dangers, and every corner, every alleyway, feels like a potential trap.

Shakira pulls the hood of her jacket up, trying to shield herself from the prying eyes of those who might recognize her. But it's no use. The streets have a long memory, and the faces Shakira encounters remember her all too well. Some look away, not wanting to be associated with her fall from grace. Others, the ones with scores to settle, watch her with twisted satisfaction, their gazes lingering just a little too long.

As Shakira walks, the whispers start. "Ain't that Shakira? She di Carnival Queen who lose everything." "Look how di mighty fall, eh?" Shakira's hands ball into fists inside her pockets, but Shakira keeps moving, forcing herself not to react. It's not worth it. Not anymore.

Shakira heads toward the market, the place where the city's underbelly thrives. This is where Shakira must go to survive, to make whatever money she can, doing whatever it takes. The vibrant stalls, once a blur of color and life, now seem muted, weighed down by the oppressive atmosphere that hangs over the market like a shroud. The vendors eye her warily as she approaches, some of them recognizing the former queen now reduced to a desperate woman scrounging for scraps.

"Look who it is," a familiar voice sneers as Shakira reaches a corner of the market where the shadows seem to gather. Shakira turns to see Rico, one of her old rivals, leaning against a wall, a smirk playing on his lips. Rico was never a fan of Shakira, always looking for ways to undermine her, and now that she's fallen, he's relishing the opportunity to twist the knife.

"Rico," Shakira says, her voice flat, devoid of the power it once held. "What yuh want?"

Rico chuckles, pushing off the wall and swaggering over to her. "I don't want nothin', Shakira. Just here to see di mighty queen on her knees. How di tables turn, eh?"

Shakira's jaw tightens, but Shakira forces herself to stay calm. She needs to find work, needs to make money, and picking a fight with Rico won't help. "I'm lookin' for work," Shakira says, cutting straight to the point. "Yuh got anythin'?"

Rico raises an eyebrow, pretending to consider it. "Work, yuh say? Ain't dat rich. Di great Shakira beggin' for work like any other street rat."

Shakira's patience wears thin, but she bites back the retort burning on her tongue. "I ain't beggin'. I'm offerin'. I still got skills, and yuh know it."

Rico's smirk fades, his eyes narrowing as he sizes her up. He's considering it, Shakira can tell, weighing the pros and cons of bringing her on board. But in the end, Rico's need to see her squirm wins out. "Nah, Shakira. I don't got nothin' for yuh. Best yuh move on before someone less friendly comes along."

The dismissal stings, but Shakira turns on her heel and walks away, forcing herself to keep her head high even though all Shakira wants to do is disappear. The market, once a place where Shakira wielded influence, now feels like a labyrinth of hostility, each step a reminder of how far she's fallen.

Shakira spends the day moving from one corner of the city to the next, trying to find work, trying to get by. But every door Shakira knocks on is slammed in her face. The people who once owed Shakira favors now avoid her, afraid of being dragged down by her sinking reputation. The ones who do speak to Shakira do so with barely disguised contempt, reminding her with every word that she's no longer the queen of anything.

As the sun dips below the horizon, casting the city in a shadowy haze, Shakira finds herself in the worst parts of town, where desperation breeds danger. The streets here are filled with those who have nothing to lose, and Shakira knows she's vulnerable. She's no longer protected by her name or her power—now, she's just another target.

Shakira slips into an alleyway, the air thick with the smell of rot and decay. Shakira's steps quicken as the alley narrows, her heart pounding in her chest. The voices of the past echo in her mind, reminding her of all the enemies she's made, all the people who would love to see her dead.

As Shakira reaches the end of the alley, she sees a group of men standing in the shadows, their eyes glinting in the dim light. Shakira's breath catches in her throat, and for a moment, Shakira considers turning back, but it's too late. One of the men steps forward, a cruel smile spreading across his face.

"Well, well, look what we have here," he says, his voice dripping with malice. "If it ain't Shakira herself, crawlin' through di gutter."

Shakira's blood runs cold, but Shakira forces herself to stand her ground. "What yuh want?" Shakira asks, her voice steady despite the fear gnawing at her insides.

The man laughs, a harsh, grating sound that sends a shiver down Shakira's spine. "What do we want? Oh, we want lots of t'ings. Payback, mostly. Yuh made a lot of enemies, Shakira, and now dat yuh got nothin', we figure it's time to collect."

The group closes in, and Shakira's heart races as she realizes there's no escape. Shakira's cornered, outnumbered, and there's no one coming to save her. Shakira's fists clench, and Shakira braces herself for the worst.

But just as the men move to strike, a voice rings out from the end of the alley. "Leave her alone."

The men pause, turning to see who's dared to interrupt. Shakira glances over, her breath catching as she recognizes the figure standing there. It's one of her old lieutenants, a man who used to run errands for her, a man Shakira thought had abandoned her like everyone else.

"Dis ain't your business," the leader of the group growls, but the newcomer steps forward, his eyes hard.

"Maybe it is," he says. "Yuh wanna get to her, yuh gotta go through me first."

The tension in the alley is palpable, the air crackling with the promise of violence. The men exchange glances, considering their next move. But after a long, tense moment, they back off, deciding that tonight isn't worth the trouble.

"Dis ain't over, Shakira," the leader spits, but the threat falls flat as they retreat into the shadows, leaving Shakira and her unexpected savior alone in the alley.

Shakira exhales a shaky breath, the adrenaline still coursing through her veins. "Why yuh help me?" Shakira asks, her voice barely above a whisper.

The man shrugs, a sad smile on his face. "Yuh were good to me, once. And even queens need someone to watch their back."

Shakira nods, too tired to argue, too grateful to question it. Shakira's lost everything, but maybe—just maybe—Shakira hasn't lost everyone.

As the two of them leave the alley and head back into the city, the night feels darker than it ever has before. Every shadow holds a threat, every corner a reminder of what Shakira's lost. Shakira knows that she can't keep living like this, always looking over her shoulder, always waiting for the next attack.

Chapter 10: A Glimmer of Hope

The night air is heavy with humidity as Shakira trudges through the empty streets of Port Antonio. The city that once shone like a beacon of power and opportunity now looms over Shakira like a prison, its shadows deep and unforgiving. Shakira's steps are slow, her body weighed down by exhaustion, but it's her mind that bears the heaviest burden. The events of the past few weeks have carved deep lines into Shakira's once-proud face, and the fire that fueled her ambition has dwindled to a mere flicker.

Shakira reaches a small park tucked away in the heart of the city, a place she used to visit when she needed to clear her head. The park is deserted now, the swings creaking softly in the breeze, the benches weathered and worn. Shakira sinks onto one of the benches, her eyes staring blankly ahead as her mind races.

The power, the wealth, the status—everything Shakira fought so hard to attain—now feels like a distant dream, a cruel joke played by fate. Shakira remembers the nights spent in lavish parties, surrounded by sycophants who praised her every move, the thrill of wielding power over men who thought they could control her. But what did it all amount to? A fall from grace so severe that Shakira is left with nothing but the clothes on her back and the bitter taste of betrayal.

Shakira's thoughts drift back to the beginning, to the girl she once was before the allure of the fast life pulled her into its orbit. Shakira had dreams once, dreams that didn't involve hustling or manipulation, dreams that were pure, untainted by the darkness that now envelops her. But those dreams were swallowed whole by the streets, replaced by a hunger for power and a need to prove herself in a world that didn't care if she lived or died.

Shakira's fists clench in her lap as she recalls the choices she made, the people she stepped on, the lives she ruined in her pursuit of the crown. Every decision, every move, every calculated risk—each one brought her closer to the edge until, finally, she toppled over, dragged down by the very forces she once thought she controlled.

A tear slips down Shakira's cheek, the first she's allowed herself since her world came crashing down. Shakira quickly wipes it away, angered by her own weakness, but the tears keep coming, each one a drop of the sorrow and regret that has been festering inside her. Shakira bends forward, burying her face in her hands as the sobs wrack her body, the weight of her losses crashing down on her all at once.

Shakira cries for the girl she used to be, for the woman she became, for the life she built and destroyed with her own hands. But as the tears flow, something begins to shift inside her, a tiny spark of clarity that cuts through the fog of despair. Shakira begins to see, with painful clarity, the true cost of the life she led. The power and wealth she craved were nothing more than a facade, a brittle mask that shattered at the first sign of weakness.

But amid the despair, Shakira starts to see a way out—a glimmer of hope that shines faintly through the darkness. Shakira's not sure where it comes from, not sure if it's real or just a desperate fantasy, but it's there, a thread of light that Shakira clings to with all her strength.

Shakira lifts her head, her tear-streaked face illuminated by the faint glow of a nearby streetlamp. Shakira's breathing slows, the sobs subsiding as Shakira forces herself to think, to plan, to find a way to pull herself out of this abyss. The streets took everything from her, but Shakira refuses to let them take her soul.

Shakira's mind races, the wheels turning as Shakira pieces together a path forward. Shakira knows she can't go back to the life she once led, can't return to the power games and manipulation that brought her to this point. But what if Shakira could use what she's learned, what she's experienced, to carve out a new path? What if there's a way to redeem herself, to make amends for the mistakes she made, to help others avoid the traps that ensnared her?

Shakira knows it won't be easy, knows that the road to redemption is long and treacherous, but it's a road she's willing to walk if it means finding peace, finding a purpose beyond the hollow pursuit of power. Shakira doesn't have much left, but she has her wits, her experience, and a resolve that hasn't been completely broken. And maybe, just maybe, that's enough.

Shakira pushes herself to her feet, the decision solidifying in her mind with every step she takes. The streets are still dangerous, still filled with enemies who would love nothing more than to see her dead, but Shakira's not afraid. Not anymore. Shakira's lived through the worst, and she's still standing.

As Shakira walks through the empty streets, the city feels different. The oppressive weight that once pressed down on her chest has lifted slightly, replaced by a sense of purpose, a determination to rise above the ashes of her former life. Shakira knows she has a long way to go, knows that the road ahead is fraught with danger, but for the first time in weeks, Shakira feels something other than despair.

Shakira reaches a small, nondescript building on the edge of the city, a place she hasn't visited in years. The sign above the door is faded, barely legible, but Shakira knows what it says: "Community Center." Shakira hesitates for a moment, her hand hovering over the door handle. Shakira's not sure if she's ready for this, not sure if she's strong enough to face the people inside, but Shakira pushes the doubts aside and opens the door.

Inside, the center is a hive of activity. Women and children bustle about, the air filled with the sounds of conversation, laughter, and the occasional cry. Shakira's heart tightens at the sight, the memories of her own childhood flashing through her mind. Shakira grew up in places like this, places that offered a glimmer of hope in a world that seemed determined to crush her.

Shakira steps inside, her eyes scanning the room until they land on a familiar face. It's Mrs. Jenkins, the woman who ran the center when

Shakira was a girl, the woman who offered her a safe haven when the streets got too rough. Mrs. Jenkins is older now, her hair grayer, her face lined with wrinkles, but there's a warmth in her eyes that hasn't faded.

Mrs. Jenkins looks up, her gaze locking onto Shakira's. For a moment, the two women just stare at each other, the weight of the years and the choices they've made hanging between them. Then, slowly, Mrs. Jenkins smiles, a small, knowing smile that sends a wave of relief washing over Shakira.

"Shakira," Mrs. Jenkins says, her voice soft but strong. "I was wonderin' when yuh'd find yuh way back here."

Shakira's throat tightens, the words she wants to say caught in her throat. But Mrs. Jenkins doesn't need her to speak—she understands. Mrs. Jenkins nods toward a group of young girls huddled together in a corner, their faces a mix of hope and fear.

"They could use someone like yuh," Mrs. Jenkins says. "Someone who knows di streets, someone who's been where dey are. Yuh ready to help?"

Shakira's heart swells with emotion, the tears threatening to spill over again. But this time, they're not tears of despair—they're tears of hope, of redemption, of the possibility of a future that's brighter than her past.

Shakira nods, her voice steady as she replies, "Yeah, Mrs. Jenkins. I'm ready."

Chapter 11: The Turning Point

The sun hangs low in the sky, casting a golden glow over the city as Shakira makes her way to the community center. The streets are quieter than usual, the hustle and bustle of the day giving way to the calm of the evening. But in Shakira's mind, there's no peace—only a storm of thoughts and emotions as she prepares for what lies ahead. This is her chance, Shakira knows, to begin again, to carve out a new path that doesn't end in the darkness of the streets.

Shakira approaches the worn building, its exterior faded and cracked, yet somehow still standing strong. The community center is a far cry from the opulence Shakira once surrounded herself with, but there's something about its humble resilience that resonates with her. Shakira takes a deep breath, steeling herself as she pushes open the door and steps inside.

The interior is bustling with activity. Women of all ages move about, some with children in tow, others gathered in small groups, talking in hushed tones. The air is thick with a mix of tension and hope—two emotions Shakira knows all too well. Shakira's heart pounds as she surveys the scene, memories flooding back of her own time spent in places like this, of the fleeting moments of safety she found within these walls.

As Shakira moves further into the center, Mrs. Jenkins, the matronly woman who oversees the place, spots her and makes her way over. Mrs. Jenkins's warm smile is a welcome sight, a small beacon of light in the sea of uncertainty that surrounds Shakira.

"Shakira," Mrs. Jenkins greets, her voice gentle yet firm, a mix of kindness and authority that puts Shakira at ease. "I'm glad yuh here. I need help here the center can pay if you help out for maybe 20 to 30 hours a week. You ready to start today?"

Shakira nods, her throat tight with emotion. "I'm ready to help, Mrs. Jenkins," Shakira says, her voice steady despite the nerves swirling in her gut. "I can't change what I done, but maybe I can help di girls here avoid di same mistakes."

Mrs. Jenkins's eyes soften, her smile widening. "Dat's all we can do, Shakira—try to make things better where we can." She glances over at a group of young girls sitting in a corner, their faces a mix of curiosity and apprehension as they watch the older women around them. "Come, I'll introduce yuh."

As Shakira approaches the group, she feels their eyes on her, sizing her up, trying to figure out who she is and what she's about. Shakira recognizes the look in their eyes—it's the same look she used to give anyone who tried to tell her what to do, the same mix of defiance and fear that kept her alive on the streets.

"Girls," Mrs. Jenkins says, her voice carrying an air of authority that commands attention. "Dis here is Shakira. She's been where y'all are now, and she's here to help."

The girls exchange glances, their expressions guarded. Shakira takes a deep breath, knowing this won't be easy. These girls have been through hell, and they're not about to trust someone just because she says she's been there too.

"I know what y'all thinkin'," Shakira begins, her voice firm yet gentle. "Who dis woman comin' in here, thinkin' she can tell us how to live? But I ain't here to preach at yuh. I'm here to tell yuh what I wish someone had told me when I was y'all age."

One of the girls, a sharp-eyed teenager with braids that frame her face, speaks up, her tone dripping with skepticism. "And what's dat? Dat we should listen to yuh 'cause yuh been around?"

Shakira meets the girl's gaze, unflinching. "Nah, not 'cause I been around. But 'cause I know what happens when yuh think yuh got it all figured out, when yuh think yuh can play di game and win. I thought I could control everything, thought I was untouchable. But look where dat got me."

Shakira gestures to herself, the worn clothes, the tired eyes, the weight of the world etched into her every line. The girls are silent, their expressions shifting as they take in her words.

"What y'all see now," Shakira continues, "ain't what I used to be. I had power, money, respect. But all dat don't mean nothin' when yuh ain't got peace in yuh heart, when yuh can't trust nobody, not even yuhself."

Another girl, younger and with a nervous energy that radiates off her, asks, "So what happened? How did yuh lose it all?"

Shakira's eyes darken, the memories of her downfall still fresh in her mind. "I trusted di wrong people, made deals wit' di devil, thought I could keep climbin' higher and higher. But di higher yuh climb, di harder yuh fall. And when yuh fall, ain't nobody there to catch yuh."

The girls are quiet, the weight of Shakira's words settling over them like a heavy blanket. Shakira can see the fear in their eyes, the realization that they're on the same path she was, that they're just a few wrong moves away from the same fate.

"I'm here to tell yuh," Shakira says, her voice steady and strong, "dat yuh don't have to go down dat road. Yuh got choices, even when it feels like yuh don't. Yuh got people here who care about yuh, who want to see yuh make it out. But yuh gotta want it too. Yuh gotta be willin' to fight for a different life."

The sharp-eyed girl, the one who spoke up first, leans back in her chair, her arms crossed over her chest. "And what if we don't know how to fight? What if we already too deep in?"

Shakira nods, understanding the fear behind the girl's words. "Den yuh start small. Yuh take one step at a time, yuh reach out to people who can help yuh, who been through it and came out the other side. And yuh keep fightin', even when it feels like yuh losin'."

The room is quiet, the girls processing what Shakira has said. Mrs. Jenkins watches from the sidelines, her eyes filled with a mix of pride and hope. She knows these girls need someone like Shakira, someone who can speak their language, who understands their struggles in a way no one else can.

After a moment, the sharp-eyed girl uncrosses her arms, her posture relaxing just a little. "So what do we do now?" she asks, her tone less defiant, more curious.

Shakira smiles, a small, genuine smile that feels foreign on her face but also right. "We start by talkin', by sharin' our stories, by learnin' from each other. Ain't nobody here gonna judge yuh. We all got our demons. But yuh gotta be willin' to face 'em, to put in di work to be better."

The girls nod slowly, some of them more reluctantly than others, but there's a shift in the room, a change in the energy. They're listening, really listening, and Shakira knows that this is the beginning of something important, something that could change not just their lives but hers as well.

Over the next few days, Shakira becomes a fixture at the community center, spending hours talking with the girls, listening to their stories, offering advice, and sharing her own experiences. The girls are still wary, still guarded, but little by little, they begin to open up, to trust her.

Shakira sees pieces of herself in each of them—the hunger for more, the desire to escape their circumstances, the fear that they're not enough. Shakira understands their pain, their anger, their desperation, and she uses her street smarts and hard-earned wisdom to guide them, to show them that there's another way.

But the work isn't easy. The girls push back, test her limits, challenge her at every turn. Shakira knows it's because they're scared, because they've been hurt too many times before. But Shakira is patient, persistent, determined to help them even when they resist.

As the days turn into weeks, the girls start to change. Their defiance softens, their walls begin to crack, and they start to believe that maybe, just maybe, they can have a future that doesn't end in tragedy. Shakira watches their transformation with a mixture of pride and humility, knowing that she's playing a part in something bigger than herself.

Shakira's journey is far from over, but for the first time in a long time, she feels like she's on the right path.

Chapter 12: Rebuilding Trust

The days pass in a blur, each one bringing Shakira deeper into the rhythms of the community center. The hustle and chaos of the streets still linger in her mind, but now, they're muted, overshadowed by the steady beat of a different kind of life. Shakira wakes up each morning with a sense of purpose that she hasn't felt in years. It's still new, still fragile, but it's there, growing stronger with each interaction, each conversation she has with the girls at the center.

Shakira walks through the front doors of the community center, the familiar creak of the old wood beneath her feet greeting her like an old friend. The air inside is warm, filled with the sounds of chatter, laughter, and the occasional outburst as the girls navigate their way through another day. Shakira feels a sense of calm settle over her, a stark contrast to the chaos that used to define her life.

As Shakira moves through the center, she's greeted by nods and smiles from the women who have come to know her, to see her as more than just the fallen queen of the Carnival. The mistrust that once lingered in their eyes has begun to fade, replaced by something Shakira hasn't seen in a long time—respect. It's a small thing, but it means the world to her.

Shakira approaches a group of girls huddled together in the corner, their voices low and conspiratorial. They stop talking as Shakira nears, their eyes watching her with a mix of curiosity and caution. Shakira recognizes the look—they're testing her, waiting to see if she's the real deal or just another person who's going to let them down.

"What y'all up to?" Shakira asks, her tone light but with an edge that commands attention.

The girls exchange glances, and then one of them, a girl named Kayla, speaks up. "We were just talkin' 'bout di block party dis weekend. Wonderin' if we should go."

Shakira nods, understanding the unspoken concerns behind Kayla's words. The block party is a big deal in their neighborhood, but it's also a magnet for trouble. Shakira knows that the girls are torn between wanting to have fun and staying out of the mess that always seems to follow these events.

"It's up to y'all," Shakira says, her voice calm. "But yuh know how these t'ings go. It might start out nice, but it can turn ugly real quick. Yuh gotta ask yuhself if it's worth it."

The girls nod, their expressions thoughtful. Shakira doesn't push them further; she knows they have to make their own decisions. But she's planted the seed, given them something to think about, and that's enough for now.

As the girls go back to their conversation, Shakira moves on, her mind already on the next task. Shakira's been spending more time at the center, volunteering for whatever needs to be done—whether it's organizing supplies, mentoring the girls, or just being a shoulder to lean on. It's not glamorous work, but it's real, and it's helping her piece together the shattered fragments of her self-worth.

Shakira's path through the center takes her to the back room, where Mrs. Jenkins is sorting through donations. The older woman looks up as Shakira enters, a smile lighting up her face.

"Shakira, just di person I wanted to see," Mrs. Jenkins says, her voice warm. "We got a new group of girls comin' in later dis afternoon. Thought yuh might want to talk to 'em, help dem settle in."

Shakira feels a pang of something close to pride, a feeling she hasn't let herself indulge in for a long time. "Of course, Mrs. Jenkins," Shakira replies. "I'd be happy to."

Mrs. Jenkins nods, her eyes filled with approval. "Yuh been doin' good work here, Shakira. People are startin' to see yuh for who yuh really are, not for who yuh used to be."

Shakira shifts on her feet, the praise making her feel both grateful and uncomfortable. Shakira's not used to people seeing her in a positive light, and it's still hard to accept that maybe, just maybe, she's doing something right.

"Thanks," Shakira says, her voice quieter than before. "But I still got a lot to make up for."

Mrs. Jenkins steps closer, placing a hand on Shakira's shoulder. "We all got our pasts, Shakira. What matters is what yuh do now, how yuh move forward. And from where I'm standin', yuh movin' in di right direction."

Shakira nods, the weight of her past still heavy, but Mrs. Jenkins's words offer a glimmer of comfort. Shakira knows she can't change what she's done, but she can keep trying to do better, to be better. And for now, that's enough.

The afternoon passes in a blur of activity. Shakira helps the new girls settle in, guiding them through the initial awkwardness and fear that comes with being in a new place. Shakira shares her own story in bits and pieces, careful not to overwhelm them but giving them just enough to know that she's been where they are, that she understands what they're going through.

The girls respond to Shakira's honesty, opening up to her in ways that surprise even her. They ask questions, some shyly, others boldly, about how she ended up at the center, about what it was like to fall from such heights. Shakira answers each question with as much truth as she can muster, knowing that these girls need to hear the reality of her situation, not some sugar-coated version.

By the time the day comes to an end, Shakira feels a deep sense of exhaustion, but it's a good kind of tired. The kind that comes from a day well spent, from knowing that she's making a difference, even if it's just a small one. Shakira's sense of self-worth is still fragile, still something she's rebuilding piece by piece, but it's there, growing stronger with each day she spends at the center.

As Shakira steps out into the evening air, the city around her feels different. The streets are still the same, still filled with the dangers and temptations that have always been there, but Shakira's perspective has shifted. Shakira's no longer walking through these streets as the disgraced Carnival Queen, but as a woman who's faced her demons and is coming out the other side, stronger and more focused than before.

Shakira's steps are more assured as she makes her way home, her thoughts no longer weighed down by the constant fear of retribution or the nagging sense of failure. Shakira's found a place where she belongs, a place where she's making a difference, and that's worth more than any crown or title she once held.

Chapter 13: A New Legacy

The early morning sun casts a warm, golden light over the streets of Port Antonio as Shakira makes her way to the community center. The city is beginning to wake, and with it, a sense of purpose fills Shakira. The chaos and pain of her past still linger in the back of her mind, but now, they are tempered by something new—a sense of responsibility, a determination to leave behind a legacy that matters.

Shakira enters the community center to find it already bustling with activity. Women and children are gathered in small groups, talking, laughing, and sharing stories. The energy is different from when Shakira first started coming here. There's a sense of hope in the air, a feeling that things might actually change for the better.

As Shakira moves through the center, she's greeted with nods of acknowledgment and respect. The skepticism that once colored the eyes of those she passed has softened, replaced by trust. These are the same people who once whispered about her behind closed doors, who shook their heads at her fall from grace. Now, they look at Shakira with something akin to admiration.

"Morning, Shakira!" a woman calls out, her voice bright and cheerful. It's Marcia, a mother of three who's been struggling to keep her kids out of trouble. Shakira helped Marcia find a job and get her kids enrolled in after-school programs. Marcia's smile is genuine, and it warms Shakira's heart.

"Morning, Marcia," Shakira replies, returning the smile. "How's everything going?"

"Better, thanks to yuh," Marcia says, her eyes shining with gratitude. "Di boys are stayin' outta trouble, and I finally got di bills under control."

Shakira nods, feeling a swell of pride. "Yuh doin' good, Marcia. Keep it up."

Marcia's smile widens, and she gives Shakira a small nod before heading off to her next task. Shakira watches her go, feeling a deep sense of satisfaction. This—helping people, making a difference—this is what she was meant to do. Not hustling, not scheming, but building something real, something lasting.

Shakira continues her rounds, checking in on the various activities happening throughout the center. In one room, she finds a group of girls working on a project for school, their faces focused and determined. In another, a few of the younger children are gathered around a table, coloring pictures and chattering excitedly.

As Shakira approaches the room where the older girls usually gather, she hears their voices, low and intense. Shakira pauses outside the door, listening for a moment before stepping inside.

The girls are huddled together, their heads bent close as they talk. When they see Shakira, they straighten up, their expressions a mix of guilt and defiance. Shakira recognizes the look—it's the same one she wore so many times in her youth, when she was plotting her next move, weighing the risks and rewards.

"What's goin' on, girls?" Shakira asks, her tone calm but firm.

The girls exchange glances, and then one of them, Kayla, speaks up. "We was just talkin' about somethin', Miss Shakira. Nothin' serious."

Shakira raises an eyebrow, not buying it for a second. "Yuh know y'all can talk to me, right? Whatever it is, I ain't here to judge."

The girls hesitate, but Shakira's patience pays off. Finally, Kayla sighs and speaks up. "Some of di older boys been talkin' 'bout a new hustle. Somethin' big. They been tryin' to get us to join in, sayin' it's easy money."

Shakira's heart sinks. She knows exactly what kind of "hustle" these boys are talking about, and she knows where it leads. Shakira steps closer, her expression serious.

"And what y'all think 'bout it?" Shakira asks, her voice low.

Kayla shrugs, but Shakira can see the uncertainty in her eyes. "I dunno. It sounds good, but...I remember what yuh said 'bout easy money, 'bout how it always comes with a cost."

Shakira nods, her heart aching for these girls who are being tempted by the same lies she once believed. "Kayla, listen to me. I been down dat road. It might seem like di answer now, but all it's gonna do is take yuh deeper into di mess. Yuh got a chance to do somethin' better, to be somethin' better. Don't let nobody take dat away from yuh."

The girls are silent, the weight of Shakira's words settling over them like a heavy blanket. Shakira can see the conflict in their eyes, the tug-of-war between wanting something better and the lure of easy money. Shakira steps back, giving them space to think.

"I ain't gonna tell yuh what to do," Shakira says, her voice gentle but firm. "But I want yuh to think 'bout what yuh really want, 'bout where yuh want to be in a year, in five years. Di decisions yuh make now are gonna shape di rest of yuh life. Don't take dat lightly."

Shakira turns to leave, but before she can step out the door, Kayla calls out to her. "Miss Shakira?"

Shakira turns back, her expression softening. "Yeah, Kayla?"

"Thanks," Kayla says, her voice quiet but sincere. "For not givin' up on us."

Shakira's throat tightens, and she nods, her voice thick with emotion. "I'll never give up on y'all. Y'all worth too much."

Shakira leaves the room, her heart heavy but hopeful. Shakira knows the path these girls are walking, knows the temptations and dangers that lie ahead. But she also knows that they're listening, that her words are reaching them. And that's enough to keep her going.

As the day goes on, Shakira finds herself thinking more and more about the legacy she's leaving behind. It's not about power or wealth anymore—those things never brought her true happiness. It's about making a difference, about helping others avoid the mistakes she made.

Shakira's influence in the neighborhood begins to grow, not because of who she was, but because of who she's becoming. People start to come to her for advice, for guidance, for help in navigating the challenges of life in the streets. Shakira's reputation shifts from that of the disgraced Carnival Queen to that of a mentor, a leader who's dedicated to making a positive impact.

The transformation isn't lost on the community. The women who once gossiped about her now speak of her with respect, the men who once dismissed her now acknowledge her wisdom. Even the younger generation, the ones who never knew her at the height of her power, start to look up to her, seeing in her a role model, someone who's been through the fire and come out the other side.

But Shakira knows that this new legacy comes with its own set of challenges. The streets are still dangerous, still full of people who want to see her fail. Shakira has to be vigilant, has to keep proving herself every day. But she's ready for it. Shakira's learned the hard way that real power doesn't come from wealth or status—it comes from within, from the choices she makes, from the people she helps.

Chapter 14: Marcus's Empire Crumbles

The air in Port Antonio is thick with tension as the balance of power in the city begins to shift. The once-mighty Marcus, who took over her empire and ruled the streets with an iron fist, now finds his empire slowly slipping from his grasp. The change is subtle at first, almost imperceptible—a missed payment here, a deal that falls through there—but the signs are there, clear to those who know where to look.

Marcus sits in the back room of a dimly lit nightclub, his usual place of business. The room reeks of sweat and stale alcohol, the air heavy with the lingering scent of cigar smoke. Marcus leans back in his chair, his eyes narrowed as he watches his men argue over the latest shipment that's gone missing. The tension is palpable, the fear in the room almost suffocating.

"Y'all better get yuh act together," Marcus growls, his voice low and dangerous. "I ain't in di mood for excuses."

The men fall silent, their eyes shifting nervously as they try to avoid Marcus's gaze. They know better than to cross him, but the cracks in his authority are beginning to show. The fear that once kept them in line is now tinged with doubt, with whispers of weakness that they dare not speak aloud.

Marcus clenches his fists, his frustration mounting. He knows something's changed, something he can't quite put his finger on. His empire, once so solid, so unshakeable, is crumbling around him, and he's powerless to stop it. Marcus's mind races, trying to figure out where it all went wrong, but all he can think about is Shakira.

Shakira, the woman he used as a pawn in his game for power. Marcus had written her off, thought she was finished, but now, she's back, and she's making waves in a way he never anticipated. Shakira's influence is spreading through the community like wildfire, her redemption story inspiring those who once feared him to rise up, to challenge his authority.

Marcus slams his fist on the table, the sound echoing through the room. "I want answers!" he barks, his voice laced with fury. "Who's been messin' wit' my business? Who's been turnin' people against me?"

The men exchange uneasy glances, but none of them dare to speak. They know the truth—that Marcus's power is slipping, that the streets are no longer his to command—but they also know that admitting it out loud would be signing their own death warrants.

One of Marcus's lieutenants, a wiry man with a scar running down the side of his face, finally speaks up. "Boss, it's Shakira," he says cautiously. "She's been talkin' to people, gettin' in their heads. People are startin' to see her as somethin' else now, not just di woman who fell from grace."

Marcus's eyes darken, his jaw tightening. "Yuh tellin' me dat people are listenin' to her now? Dat they think she's some kinda savior?"

The lieutenant nods, his eyes downcast. "It's not just talk, boss. She's been helpin' people, givin' them hope. Di things yuh used to control, she's been changin' dem. And people are startin' to think maybe, just maybe, dey don't need yuh or this kinda life no more."

Marcus's anger flares, hot and violent. The idea that Shakira, the woman he betrayed and left for dead, could be the one to bring him down is almost too much for him to bear. Marcus's hand itches for his gun, the urge to silence this insolence burning in his veins, but he knows that killing his men won't solve the problem.

Instead, Marcus stands up, his movements slow and deliberate. "We're goin' to remind di streets who runs dis city," he says, his voice deadly calm. "We're goin' to show dem what happens when dey forget who holds di power."

Marcus storms out of the nightclub, his men scrambling to follow. The night is still young, and there's work to be done—deals to be made, threats to be enforced. Marcus's mind is a whirlwind of rage and determination as he makes his way through the city, his every step a calculated move to reclaim what's slipping away.

But the streets have changed. The people who once cowered before him now look at him with something else in their eyes—something that feels dangerously close to defiance. Marcus notices the subtle shifts in the way people speak to him, the way they no longer rush to do his bidding. It's like the fear that once ruled their lives has been replaced by something stronger, something he can't control.

It's not long before Marcus's suspicions are confirmed. Word spreads quickly on the streets, whispers that Shakira's influence is growing, that she's becoming a beacon of hope in a community that's been crushed under the weight of his tyranny for too long. The rumors that Marcus used to brush off as idle gossip now take on a new weight, a new significance that he can't ignore.

Marcus's empire is crumbling, and Shakira is at the center of it all.

Desperate to regain control, Marcus begins to crack down on the people he once trusted. He demands loyalty, ruthlessly rooting out anyone he suspects of turning against him. The atmosphere grows tense, paranoia creeping into every corner of his organization. The loyalty Marcus once commanded through fear now breeds resentment, and the more he tightens his grip, the more his power slips away.

The final blow comes one night when Marcus's crew fails to show up for a critical meeting. It's the kind of betrayal that Marcus never saw coming, the kind that leaves him reeling, questioning everything he thought he knew. The people who once swore loyalty to him have deserted him, leaving him alone to face the consequences of his actions.

As Marcus sits alone, the reality of his situation finally sinks in. He's lost control. His empire, once vast and unchallenged, has been brought to its knees by a woman he thought he'd broken. Shakira's redemption has become Marcus's downfall, her influence spreading through the community like a virus, infecting everything he once held dear.

Marcus stares out the window at the city below, his mind racing as he tries to come up with a plan to regain his power. But deep down, he knows it's too late. The people no longer fear him, no longer respect him, and without that, he has nothing. Marcus's grip on the streets has weakened, and the empire he built through blood and fear is crumbling around him.

Chapter 15: Confronting Marcus

The night air is thick with tension as Shakira walks through the narrow streets of Port Antonio, her mind a whirlwind of emotions. The confrontation with Marcus is inevitable—has been since the moment she decided to reclaim her life. But tonight, the stakes are higher than ever she is going to confront Marcus for trying to destroy her and for continuing to try to destroy those she sees and helps every day. Shakira knows that this is the final stand, the moment that will determine whether she will truly be free from the shadow of her past.

Shakira's steps are steady, her resolve unshakable as she makes her way to the abandoned warehouse on the outskirts of the city. The place is a relic of another time, its walls crumbling and graffiti-covered, a testament to the decay that has seeped into every corner of the streets. It's the perfect place for a showdown—hidden from prying eyes, far from the hustle and bustle of the city center.

As Shakira approaches the entrance, she sees the dim glow of a single lightbulb hanging from a wire inside. The air is heavy with the scent of dust and mildew, a reminder of how far she's come from the life she once knew. Shakira pauses for a moment, taking a deep breath to steady herself before pushing open the rusted door.

Inside, the warehouse is as desolate as she expected—empty crates and broken machinery litter the floor, casting long shadows in the dim light. At the far end of the room, Marcus stands with his back to her, his silhouette outlined against the flickering bulb. He's alone, his usual entourage nowhere in sight—a sign that even his closest allies have deserted him.

Shakira takes a few steps forward, her heels clicking against the concrete floor, the sound echoing through the cavernous space. Marcus turns at the sound, his eyes narrowing as they meet hers. There's no fear in his gaze, only anger—a burning, seething rage that simmers beneath the surface.

"So, yuh finally decided to show up," Marcus sneers, his voice dripping with contempt. "Yuh think yuh can just waltz in here like you still own these streets?"

Shakira doesn't flinch, doesn't back down. Instead, she meets Marcus's gaze head-on, her expression calm and controlled. "Dis was never yours, Marcus. Yuh took it by force. But di people don't care no more. I don't care nor more."

Marcus's jaw tightens, his hands clenching into fists at his sides. "Yuh don't know what yuh talkin' 'bout. I built dis empire from nothin', and yuh think yuh can just come in and tear it down?"

Shakira takes another step forward, closing the distance between them. "Yuh built it on lies, on pain, on di backs of di people yuh used and discarded. But dat's over now. Di people see yuh for what yuh really are —a coward who hides behind threats and deceit 'cause yuh too weak to stand on yuh own."

Marcus's eyes flash with fury, his body tensing as if he's about to lash out. But Shakira stands her ground, refusing to be intimidated. She's faced worse than Marcus in her time, and she's come out the other side stronger for it.

"Yuh ain't nothin' without di bullshit yuh spread," Shakira continues, her voice steady and unyielding. "And now dat di people no care, yuh ain't got nothin' left. Yuh empire is crumblin', Marcus, and yuh know it."

Marcus lets out a low, humorless laugh, shaking his head as if he can't believe what he's hearing. "Yuh really believe that, Shakira? Yuh think I would let up that easy?"

Shakira's eyes narrow, her voice dropping to a dangerous whisper. "Yea I believe it, Marcus. Nobody give a fuck about you especially me."

The words hang in the air, heavy with finality. Marcus's smirk falters, his confidence shaken by the certainty in Shakira's voice. He looks around the empty warehouse, as if searching for some sign of the power he once wielded, but there's nothing left—nothing but the ghosts of his past and the bitter taste of defeat.

Shakira steps even closer, so close now that she can see the beads of sweat forming on Marcus's brow, the way his hands tremble ever so slightly at his sides. "It's over, Marcus," Shakira says, her tone firm and resolute. "Yuh lost. Di people have already turned against yuh, and there's nothin' yuh can do to change dat."

Marcus's face contorts with rage, his voice rising in desperation. "I can get rid of you, Shakira! Don't think I won't!"

But Shakira just shakes her head, pity filling her eyes as she looks at the man who once held so much power over her life. "Yuh can't hurt me no more, Marcus. I ain't afraid of yuh, and neither are di people. Di only person yuh hurtin' now is yuhself."

For a moment, there's silence between them, the tension in the air almost suffocating. Marcus's chest rises and falls with each labored breath, his eyes filled with a mixture of fury and disbelief. Shakira watches him, her expression unreadable, but there's a strength in her stance that wasn't there before.

Finally, Marcus's shoulders slump, the fight draining out of him as the reality of his defeat sinks in. He looks at Shakira, and for the first time, there's no hatred in his gaze—only a hollow emptiness, a man who's lost and knows it.

"Yuh really think yuh can run shit after all dis?" Marcus asks, his voice tinged with bitterness. "Yuh think di people will just forget what yuh did, what yuh used to be?"

Shakira's lips curve into a small, sad smile. "I don't need dem to forget, Marcus. I just need dem to see dat I've changed, dat I'm tryin' to make things right. And dey will, in time. Dey already are."

Marcus shakes his head, his eyes dark with defeat. "Yuh a fool, Shakira. Dis world don't let people like us change. Dis life don't let go dat easy."

Shakira's smile fades, her expression turning serious. "Maybe so. But I'd rather die tryin' to be somethin' better than live as di monster I used to be."

Marcus's eyes flicker with something—regret, perhaps, or maybe just the realization that he's lost. He nods once, a sharp, bitter motion, and then turns away, his footsteps heavy as he walks toward the exit.

As Marcus reaches the door, he pauses, glancing back at Shakira one last time. "Fuck you bitch, his voice low and menacing. "Yuh might have di upper hand now, but don't think for a second dat I won't be back."

But Shakira just nods, her expression calm and resolute. "We'll see, Marcus. We'll see."

With that, Marcus steps out into the night, the door slamming shut behind him with a finality that echoes through the empty warehouse. Shakira stands there for a moment, letting the silence settle around her, feeling the weight of what's just happened.

It's over. Marcus is gone, as quick as he had come and ruined her life he was gone just as fast.

But even as Shakira steps out into the cool night air, there's a lingering unease in her chest—a feeling that this victory, hard-won as it is, might not be the end. The streets are still dangerous, still filled with people who would see her fall, and Shakira knows she can't let her guard down. Not yet.

Chapter 16: The Carnival of Redemption

The early morning sun casts a golden hue over Port Antonio, as the city awakens to the rhythmic sounds of the Caribbean Carnival. The air is electric with excitement, the scent of street food mingling with the sweet aroma of flowers and the distant hum of soca music. The streets are alive with color and movement, a vibrant tapestry of costumes, laughter, and celebration. It's the same festival that Shakira once ruled with an iron grip, but now, everything has changed.

Shakira stands at the edge of the bustling street, her heart beating in time with the drums that echo through the air. The Carnival is in full swing, and the energy is palpable—infectious even. But Shakira is no longer the queen of this world. She's no longer the center of attention, no longer the woman everyone feared or envied. Shakira watches from the sidelines now, content with her place in the shadows.

As Shakira takes in the sights and sounds of the festival, she feels a sense of peace settle over her—a peace she hasn't known in a long time. The chaos, the hunger for power, the endless chase for wealth—it's all behind her now. Shakira's no longer driven by those things, no longer consumed by the need to control everything around her. Instead, she finds herself smiling at the simple joys unfolding before her eyes.

Children dart through the crowd, their laughter ringing out as they chase each other with colorful streamers. Couples dance in the streets, lost in the rhythm of the music, their bodies swaying together in perfect harmony. Vendors call out to passersby, their tables piled high with vibrant fabrics, beaded jewelry, and handcrafted masks. The festival is a living, breathing entity, pulsing with life and joy, and for the first time, Shakira feels like she's truly a part of it—not as its ruler, but as a witness to its beauty.

As Shakira moves through the crowd, she catches sight of familiar faces—people she once knew, people who once feared her, now smiling and laughing, free from the weight of her past reign. There's a pang of something close to regret in Shakira's chest, but it's fleeting, quickly replaced by a quiet acceptance. Shakira knows she can't change the past, but she's making peace with it, one step at a time.

Shakira's journey takes her to a small square, where a group of women are setting up a booth for the community center. The sight warms Shakira's heart—this center, this place that has become her sanctuary, her purpose. The women greet Shakira with warm smiles and nods of acknowledgment, their respect for her evident in their eyes. They see her not as the disgraced Carnival Queen, but as a woman who has found her way back to the light.

"Morning, Miss Shakira," one of the women says, her voice filled with warmth. "Yuh here to help out today?"

Shakira smiles, the simple act bringing her more joy than she ever thought possible. "I was t'inkin' I might just watch today," Shakira replies, her tone light. "But if yuh need me, yuh know I'm here."

The woman nods, her smile widening. "We know. Yuh done plenty already. Today, yuh should enjoy di festival."

Shakira's smile lingers as she watches the women set up their booth, arranging flyers, pamphlets, and small crafts the girls at the center have made. Shakira can't help but feel a swell of pride—these women, these girls, they're part of her new legacy, a testament to the changes she's made in her life. Shakira's no longer the queen of the Carnival, but she's found something far more valuable—purpose.

As the day wears on, Shakira continues to weave through the crowd, her presence quiet and unassuming. Shakira's not seeking attention, not looking to reclaim her throne. Instead, she finds herself drawn to the simple moments—the laughter of a child, the rhythm of a drumbeat, the flash of a dancer's costume as they twirl in the street. Shakira takes it all in, savoring each moment, each sensation.

But even as Shakira revels in the joy around her, there's a lingering unease in the back of her mind. The Carnival, with all its beauty and vibrancy, is also a reminder of what she once had, of the power she once wielded. It's a reminder of the darkness that still lurks in the corners of her heart, the shadows of her past that she's still trying to outrun.

As the sun begins to dip below the horizon, casting long shadows over the city, Shakira finds herself standing at the edge of the parade route. The music has reached a fever pitch, the dancers spinning and twirling in a blur of color and motion. The crowd is thick with bodies, all pressing forward to catch a glimpse of the spectacle.

Shakira stands alone, her gaze fixed on the parade, her mind awash with memories. This was once her domain, her kingdom. Shakira remembers the feeling of power, of control, the way the crowd would part for her, the way the men would fall at her feet. But now, as she watches from the sidelines, Shakira feels none of that old desire, none of that hunger for dominance. Instead, she feels something far more precious—contentment.

Shakira's not the woman she once was. She's changed, grown, evolved. The Carnival, once a symbol of her reign, is now a symbol of her redemption. Shakira watches the parade with a sense of closure, knowing that she's finally free from the chains that once bound her.

But even as Shakira finds peace in the moment, there's still a part of her that remains vigilant, a part of her that knows the streets are never truly safe. The shadows of her past may be fading, but they're not gone. Shakira knows she must stay strong, must keep moving forward, if she's to maintain the peace she's worked so hard to achieve.

As the final float passes by, its bright lights casting a glow over the crowd, Shakira turns to leave. She walks away from the parade, her steps steady and sure, her heart lighter than it's been in years. Shakira's no longer the queen, no longer the woman everyone feared. She's something else now—something stronger, something more resilient.

Shakira's journey has come full circle. The Carnival, once a symbol of her power, is now a symbol of her redemption. Shakira knows she can't change the past, but she's found a way to make peace with it, to use it as a foundation for something new, something better.

As Shakira turns to leave, the city behind her, the reader is left with a sense of closure, a sense that Shakira has finally found her place in the world. The chapter ends on a note of quiet triumph, with the promise of a new beginning on the horizon.

Chapter 17: Reflecting on the Past

The night is alive with the sounds of the Caribbean Carnival—music pulsing through the air, the distant laughter of revelers, the rhythmic beat of drums echoing down the crowded streets. Shakira stands alone on a quiet balcony overlooking the festival, the city a vibrant sea of lights and movement beneath her. The celebration fills the air with an intoxicating energy, but Shakira feels a different kind of intensity within her—a storm of emotions she can't easily shake.

Shakira grips the iron railing, her fingers tightening as memories flood her mind. The Carnival, once the stage for her reign, is now a mirror reflecting her journey, each beat of the drum a reminder of what she's lost, what she's gained, and everything in between. The life she once knew, the power she once held, it's all gone now, washed away like the tide. But the lessons—the hard, bitter lessons—those remain etched into her soul, shaping the woman she's become.

As Shakira gazes down at the throngs of people, she's reminded of the first time she truly felt in control. The streets had been hers, and the Carnival was her playground. Shakira remembers the rush of power, the thrill of being feared and respected, of bending the will of others to match her own. But with that power came the darkness—choices that led her down a path of betrayal, greed, and loss. Shakira's breath catches in her throat as the weight of those choices settles heavy on her chest.

Shakira's thoughts drift to Marcus, the man who played such a pivotal role in her downfall. He had been her equal in so many ways—dangerous, cunning, and ruthless. Marcus had seen through her bravado, had known exactly how to exploit her weaknesses. Shakira can still see his cold eyes, the way he'd smiled as he tore everything she'd built apart. There was a time when she wanted nothing more than to see him destroyed, to watch as his empire crumbled beneath him. And now, it has. But the satisfaction she expected to feel never came.

Instead, there's only a hollow ache, a reminder of the price she paid to survive.

The wind picks up, cool against her skin, as Shakira closes her eyes and lets the memories take her. Shakira remembers the endless nights, the deals made in back rooms, the whispered promises that led to betrayal. She remembers Tasha's warning looks, the way her closest ally had tried to steer her away from the edge, only to be pushed aside when Shakira refused to listen. The regret is sharp, like a knife twisting in her gut, but Shakira knows it's too late to change what's already done.

Shakira opens her eyes, staring out at the colorful chaos below. The dancers twirl in their elaborate costumes, the music grows louder, and the people move as one, lost in the rhythm of the night. They're free, for now, from the worries that plague their daily lives. Shakira envies them, even as she knows she's finally found a different kind of freedom—a freedom that comes with understanding the past and accepting it.

Shakira's mind drifts to the women she's helped at the community center, the young girls who looked to her for guidance. Shakira had seen herself in them—the same hunger for more, the same willingness to take risks. But she'd also seen the dangers, the pitfalls they were too young to recognize. Shakira had taken it upon herself to teach them, to show them a different way, to offer them a chance she never had. It was this work that had given her life new meaning, that had helped her find redemption in the ruins of her past.

As Shakira reflects on the journey that brought her to this point, she feels a strange mix of emotions. There's pride in what she's accomplished, in the way she's turned her life around. But there's also sorrow, a deep, aching sorrow for the girl she once was, the girl who thought she could conquer the world and lost everything in the process. The pain is still there, lurking in the corners of her mind, but it's no longer all-consuming. Shakira has learned to live with it, to let it be a part of her without letting it define her.

Shakira turns her gaze to the horizon, where the first hints of dawn are beginning to break. The sky is a canvas of deep purples and blues, the stars slowly fading as the sun prepares to rise. It's a new day, a new beginning, and Shakira knows she has a choice—to let the past hold her back or to use it as fuel to keep moving forward. The decision is not an easy one, but it's one she's made before, one she will continue to make every day for the rest of her life.

Shakira thinks about the power she once craved, the wealth she once thought would make her invincible. None of it had brought her happiness, none of it had given her what she truly needed. It took losing everything for Shakira to realize that what she'd been searching for was something she already had within her—a strength, a resilience that had carried her through the darkest times. Shakira had been broken, but she'd rebuilt herself stronger, wiser, and more determined than ever.

The carnival music begins to fade as the night draws to a close, the revelers slowly dispersing as exhaustion sets in. Shakira watches them go, her heart heavy with the knowledge that the world she once dominated is now a world she can never return to. But she's okay with that. Shakira has found peace in knowing that she's made a difference, that she's helped others avoid the traps that ensnared her. Shakira's no longer seeking redemption—she's living it, every day, in the choices she makes, in the lives she touches.

As the first rays of sunlight pierce the sky, Shakira takes a deep breath, letting the cool morning air fill her lungs. The future is uncertain, the road ahead still filled with challenges, but Shakira's ready to face them. She's no longer the Carnival Queen, no longer the woman who ruled through fear and manipulation. Shakira's something else now—something better.

Chapter 18: Closure

The late afternoon sun casts long shadows over the streets of Port Antonio, the golden light bathing the city in a warm, almost nostalgic glow. Shakira walks slowly, her steps measured, as if she's taking in every detail of the world around her. The streets that once buzzed with her power and influence now feel different, softer somehow, as if they too have let go of the hold they once had on her.

Shakira pauses at the corner of a busy intersection, watching as life goes on around her. The vendors peddling their wares, the children playing in the street, the men and women going about their day—it's all so familiar, yet so distant. Shakira feels like a spectator in a life that once consumed her, a life that she's finally left behind.

As Shakira continues her walk, she finds herself passing by places that once held significance in her old life. The nightclub where she made deals that shaped the city's underworld, the boutique where she spent thousands on designer clothes and jewelry, the high-end restaurant where she entertained politicians and businessmen, securing their loyalty with charm and power. These were the places that defined her, that built the reputation of the Carnival Queen. But now, they're just memories, remnants of a past she's finally ready to let go.

Shakira stops in front of a rundown building, its windows boarded up, the paint peeling from the walls. It's a stark contrast to the luxury she once surrounded herself with, but it holds a special place in her heart. This was the first place she called home when she came to Port Antonio, a small, cramped apartment that she shared with three other girls, all of them hustling to survive. It was here that Shakira learned the rules of the streets, learned how to navigate the dangerous waters that would eventually lead her to the top.

Shakira stands there for a long moment, her mind flooded with memories of those early days—the fear, the excitement, the desperation. She remembers the nights spent plotting her next move, the hunger for more that drove her to take risks, to climb the ladder no matter the cost. Shakira can almost see her younger self, full of ambition and fire, ready to take on the world.

But that girl is gone now, replaced by a woman who has seen the other side of power, who has paid the price for her ambition. Shakira feels a pang of sadness, a mourning for the life she could have had if she had made different choices. But it's a fleeting feeling, quickly replaced by a sense of peace. Shakira knows she can't change the past, but she's finally at peace with it, finally ready to move on.

Shakira turns away from the building, leaving behind the memories that once held her captive. She walks toward the community center, the place that has become her sanctuary, her refuge from the chaos of the streets. As she approaches, she sees a group of young girls gathered outside, their laughter echoing through the air. They see her and wave, their faces lighting up with smiles. Shakira waves back, her heart swelling with pride.

Inside the community center, Shakira is greeted with the warmth and familiarity that she's come to cherish. The women she's helped, the girls she's mentored, they all see her as a beacon of hope, a symbol of strength and resilience. Shakira moves through the space, checking in on the different activities, offering advice, and sharing words of encouragement.

In one corner of the room, she finds Marcia, the young mother she helped a few weeks ago, working on a project with her children. Marcia looks up as Shakira approaches, her face breaking into a wide smile.

"Miss Shakira!" Marcia exclaims, her voice filled with gratitude. "Yuh been such a blessin' to us. I don't know how we woulda managed without yuh."

Shakira smiles, feeling a warmth in her chest that has nothing to do with the sun streaming through the windows. "Yuh doin' all di hard work, Marcia. I'm just here to help yuh along di way."

Marcia shakes her head, her eyes glistening with emotion. "It's more dan dat, Miss Shakira. Yuh gave us hope when we had none. Yuh showed us dat we can do better, dat we can be better."

Shakira's smile falters slightly, a wave of emotion washing over her. She never thought she'd be in this position, never thought she'd be the one giving hope to others. But as she looks at Marcia and her children, she realizes that this is what true power feels like—not control or fear, but the ability to lift others up, to help them find their way.

As the day turns to evening, the community center fills with the sounds of laughter and conversation, the air thick with the scent of home-cooked meals being shared among friends. Shakira takes a seat in the corner, watching the scene unfold around her. She feels a deep sense of contentment, a feeling that she's finally found her place in the world.

As the night wears on, Shakira finds herself outside once again, the cool breeze ruffling her hair as she walks through the quiet streets. The city is winding down, the chaos of the day giving way to the stillness of the night. Shakira walks with purpose, her steps sure and steady as she heads toward the edge of the city.

Shakira stops at a familiar spot, a cliff overlooking the ocean, the waves crashing against the rocks below. This is where she used to come to think, to plot her next move, to escape the pressures of her life. But tonight, it's different. Tonight, Shakira stands there not as the Carnival Queen, but as a woman who has finally found peace.

Shakira takes a deep breath, the salty air filling her lungs, and she closes her eyes, letting the sound of the waves wash over her. Shakira's mind is quiet, free from the noise that once consumed her. Shakira knows that she's finally free from the chains of her past, finally at peace with the choices she's made.

As Shakira opens her eyes, she looks out at the horizon, the first light of dawn just beginning to break through the darkness. It's a new day, a new beginning, and Shakira is ready to embrace it.

Chapter 19: A New Beginning

The morning sun casts a soft glow over Port Antonio, bathing the city in warm, golden light. The air is cool and crisp, carrying the scent of the ocean, mingling with the faint aroma of breakfast cooking in the nearby houses. The streets are still quiet, the city just beginning to wake up, but for Shakira, the day has already begun.

Shakira stands in front of the community center, the place that has become the heart of her new life. The building is modest, its exterior worn and weathered, but inside, it's a sanctuary—a place of hope and healing for those who need it most. Shakira takes a deep breath, feeling the weight of responsibility settle on her shoulders. This is her new world, a far cry from the glitz and glamour of the Carnival, but it's a world she's chosen, a world that gives her life meaning.

Shakira pushes open the door to the center, the familiar creak of the hinges greeting her like an old friend. Inside, the center is already buzzing with activity. The volunteers are setting up for the day, arranging chairs, preparing food, and organizing supplies. The energy in the room is palpable, a stark contrast to the heavy, oppressive atmosphere that once surrounded her.

As Shakira moves through the space, she's greeted with smiles and nods of acknowledgment. The people here know her, respect her, not as the Carnival Queen, but as Shakira—the woman who turned her life around, the woman who's dedicated herself to helping others do the same.

"Morning, Miss Shakira," calls out a young woman from across the room. It's Marcia, the young mother who Shakira helped get back on her feet. Marcia's face lights up as she sees Shakira, her gratitude evident in her warm smile. "Yuh ready for another busy day?"

Shakira returns the smile, feeling a sense of pride swell in her chest. "Always ready, Marcia. Yuh know me—can't keep still for too long."

Marcia laughs, a sound that's filled with genuine joy. "Dat's di truth. Yuh always movin', always helpin'. We don't know what we'd do without yuh."

Shakira waves off the compliment, but inside, it means more to her than she can express. It's these moments, these connections, that make all the difference. Shakira's no longer seeking power or wealth—she's found something far more valuable: purpose.

As the day unfolds, Shakira dives into her work. She helps organize a clothing drive, assists with food distribution, and spends time mentoring the young girls who come to the center for guidance. Each interaction, each moment, is a step further away from the life she once led, a life that seems like a distant memory now.

In the afternoon, Shakira takes a break, stepping outside to catch her breath. The sun is high in the sky now, casting sharp shadows across the pavement. Shakira leans against the wall of the building, closing her eyes as she lets the warmth of the sun soak into her skin.

As Shakira stands there, she reflects on how far she's come. The girl who once ruled the Carnival with an iron fist, who lived for the thrill of the hustle, is gone. In her place is a woman who's found peace, who's found a way to use her past to build something better. Shakira knows she can't change the choices she made, but she's found a way to make them matter, to turn them into something positive.

A noise from down the street pulls Shakira from her thoughts. She opens her eyes to see a group of young men approaching, their eyes scanning the area with an intensity that sets Shakira on edge. They're dressed in the uniform of the streets—baggy jeans, oversized hoodies, and baseball caps pulled low over their faces. It's a look Shakira knows all too well.

As the men get closer, Shakira straightens, her instincts kicking in. She's no stranger to confrontation, but this time, it's different. Shakira's not here to fight—she's here to protect what she's built, to protect the people who've come to rely on her.

The leader of the group, a tall, muscular man with a scar running down the side of his face, stops in front of Shakira, his eyes narrowing as he looks her up and down. There's a moment of tension, the air thick with unspoken words, before he finally speaks.

"So yuh di famous Shakira we been hearin' 'bout," he says, his voice low and dangerous. "Heard yuh been causin' some trouble, tryin' to change di game."

Shakira meets his gaze, her expression calm and unflinching. "I ain't tryin' to change di game. I'm tryin' to give people a choice—somethin' I never had."

The man's lips curl into a sneer. "Yuh think yuh better than us now? Just 'cause yuh got a new life, a new role to play?"

Shakira shakes her head, her voice steady. "I ain't better than nobody. I made my mistakes, paid di price. But I learned from it, and now I'm tryin' to make things right. If yuh can't respect dat, den yuh got a problem with yuhself, not me."

The man's sneer falters, a flicker of uncertainty crossing his face. He wasn't expecting this—wasn't expecting Shakira to stand her ground, to speak with such conviction. The men behind him shift uncomfortably, glancing at each other as if unsure how to proceed.

Shakira takes a step forward, her voice firm. "Dis center, dis place, it's for di people who want somethin' better. If yuh here to cause trouble, yuh can leave. But if yuh here to talk, to figure out how we can help each other, den we can sit down and have a conversation like adults."

There's a long moment of silence, the tension hanging heavy in the air. Shakira can feel the weight of the man's gaze, the challenge in his eyes. But she doesn't back down, doesn't waver. She's faced worse than this—survived worse than this.

Finally, the man lets out a low chuckle, shaking his head. "Yuh somethin' else, Shakira. Maybe yuh really have changed."

Shakira nods, her expression softening just a fraction. "We all got di chance to change, if we want it. Di question is, what yuh gonna do wit' it?"

The man studies her for a moment longer before he finally nods. "Alright. We'll talk."

Shakira gestures toward the entrance of the center. "Den let's go inside. We got a lot to discuss."

As the group follows Shakira into the building, the sense of unease that had settled over the day begins to lift. Shakira knows this is just the beginning—a new chapter in her life, one that's filled with challenges and uncertainties. But she's ready for it, ready to face whatever comes next.

Chapter 20: Legacy

The day begins with a quiet stillness, the kind that holds the promise of something new. Shakira stands by the window of the community center, looking out over the street that is just beginning to stir with life. The sun is rising, casting a soft glow over the worn buildings, the cracked sidewalks, and the few early risers making their way through the neighborhood. The same streets that once echoed her name, feared and revered her, now seem almost peaceful. Shakira takes a deep breath, feeling a sense of calm she's rarely known.

Inside the community center, the sounds of morning activity start to build—distant laughter, the clatter of chairs being arranged, the hum of conversation. The center has become Shakira's sanctuary, a place where she's found purpose beyond the streets, beyond the power she once wielded. But today feels different, heavier somehow, as if the past, present, and future are all converging in this single moment.

Shakira turns away from the window, her eyes sweeping over the room. The young girls, the ones she's taken under her wing, are gathered in a circle, their faces bright with anticipation and hope. They're different from the girls Shakira once knew—different from the girl she once was. These girls still have their innocence, still believe in possibilities, and that's what Shakira has been working to protect.

"Miss Shakira," one of the girls, a bright-eyed teenager named Kiana, calls out, breaking into her thoughts. "Yuh coming to join us?"

Shakira smiles, the kind of smile that comes from deep within, one that carries the weight of experience and the lightness of hope. "Yah, I'm coming," she replies, her voice steady and warm.

As Shakira makes her way over to the group, she takes a moment to study each of the girls—Kiana, with her infectious energy; Leila, quiet but with a fire in her eyes; Tamara, tough on the outside but tender underneath. Shakira sees pieces of herself in each of them, the same drive, the same hunger for something more, but without the darkness that once consumed her.

The girls make space for Shakira in the circle, their chatter slowing as she settles in beside them. Shakira looks around at the expectant faces, the girls waiting for her to speak, to share some wisdom, some insight that might guide them through the challenges they face.

"Yuh know," Shakira begins, her tone reflective, "I been where yuh all are now. I know di temptations, di struggles. But I also know di power of choice, di power of sayin' 'no' to di wrong path."

The girls listen intently, their eyes locked on Shakira, absorbing every word. Shakira's voice carries the weight of lived experience, of lessons learned the hard way, but also the promise of something better. It's not just about avoiding mistakes, Shakira realizes—it's about seeing the possibilities beyond the immediate, the long game rather than the quick win.

"Di streets, dey'll always be there, callin' yuh, temptin' yuh. But yuh gotta remember, yuh stronger dan dat. Yuh don't have to go down di same road I did," Shakira continues, her voice gaining strength as she speaks. "Yuh can make a different choice, build a different life."

Kiana, who has always been the most outspoken of the group, leans forward, her brow furrowed in thought. "But Miss Shakira, how do yuh know yuh makin' di right choice? How do yuh know yuh not gonna end up in di same place?"

Shakira pauses, considering the question. It's a question she's asked herself countless times, one that doesn't have a simple answer. "Yuh don't always know," Shakira admits, her tone softening. "But yuh gotta trust yuhself, trust di path yuh on. And if yuh find yuhself slippin', yuh gotta be strong enough to pull yuhself back. It's not easy, but it's worth it."

Leila, the quiet one, speaks up, her voice tentative but clear. "Yuh think we can really make it, Miss Shakira? Yuh think we can be different?"

Shakira meets Leila's gaze, seeing the uncertainty and fear that lie beneath the surface. "I know yuh can," Shakira says firmly. "Yuh already are. Yuh here, yuh listenin', yuh learnin'. Dat's di first step. Di rest, it's up to yuh, but yuh don't have to do it alone. Yuh got each other, yuh got me, and yuh got di strength to make it."

The room falls silent, the weight of Shakira's words settling over the group. It's a heavy responsibility, one that Shakira has carried alone for so long, but now she's ready to share it. She's no longer the Carnival Queen, no longer driven by the need for power or control. Her legacy isn't in the wealth she amassed or the influence she wielded—it's in the lives she's helping to change, the girls who will go on to make better choices, to live better lives.

As the day progresses, Shakira watches the girls as they go about their activities—crafts, discussions, a dance rehearsal for an upcoming event. Shakira sees the potential in each of them, the spark that could either be nurtured into something beautiful or snuffed out by the harsh realities of the world outside. Shakira knows that she can't save them all, but if she can help even one of them find a better path, then her work, her journey, has been worth it.

Later, as the day winds down, Shakira finds herself alone in the center, the girls having gone home, the volunteers cleaning up after a long day. Shakira stands in the middle of the room, the silence heavy but comforting. She thinks about the road that brought her here, the choices that led her to this place of redemption.

Shakira's mind drifts back to the streets, to the power she once held, the respect she commanded. It was intoxicating, addictive, but it was also empty, a hollow existence that left her with nothing but regrets. Now, as Shakira looks around the room, she realizes that she's finally filled that emptiness with something real, something lasting.

Shakira walks over to the window, looking out at the darkening sky. The city is settling into the night, the streetlights flickering on, casting a warm glow over the neighborhood. Shakira feels a sense of closure, a feeling that she's finally made peace with her past, finally found a way to use it to build something meaningful. She may not be Queen of the Carnival, but she was indeed still very much a Queen.

Don't miss out!

Visit the website below and you can sign up to receive emails whenever Rachael Reed publishes a new book. There's no charge and no obligation.

https://books2read.com/r/B-A-WXARB-GOCZE

BOOKS2READ

Connecting independent readers to independent writers.

Did you love *Queen of the Carnival*? Then you should read *SIS*[1] by Rachael Reed!

Sis: A Tale of Power and Betrayal

In the heart of Richmond's unforgiving streets, Jasmine has clawed her way to the top, ruling her empire with an iron fist and a sharp mind. Born into the harsh realities of the ghetto, she turned to the drug game to escape poverty, becoming a formidable force in a world dominated by betrayal, violence, and survival. But power comes at a price, and the streets are always hungry for blood.

Jasmine's journey is one of relentless ambition and ruthless determination. From small-time hustling to partnering with the notorious Dre, she learned the rules of the game the hard way. When Dre's betrayal threatened everything she had built, Jasmine took

---

1. https://books2read.com/u/mZlxoR

2. https://books2read.com/u/mZlxoR

matters into her own hands, proving that she's not one to be crossed. Now, as the queen of Richmond's underworld, she faces new enemies and internal power struggles that could bring her empire crashing down.

As Jasmine fights to maintain her reign, she grapples with the personal cost of her decisions. Guilt, regret, and the loss of innocence weigh heavily on her, even as she seeks redemption by giving back to her community. But the streets are relentless, and new threats emerge, testing her strategic brilliance and unyielding resolve.

In a world where trust is a luxury and betrayal lurks around every corner, Jasmine must navigate the treacherous waters of the drug game with cunning and ferocity. The final showdown with a new rival threatens to dismantle everything she has fought for, leading to an explosive climax that will decide the future of her reign.

Sis is a gripping tale of power, survival, and the brutal realities of urban life. With its gritty dialogue, dark undertones, and relentless pace, this novel plunges you into the heart of the streets, where every decision can mean the difference between life and death. Jasmine's story is one of fierce loyalty, calculated moves, and the constant struggle to stay on top in a world that never truly lets go.

Also by Rachael Reed

Sis
Sis 2 Blood on the Streets

Standalone
Codefendant
Codefendant
Once a Cheater
Once a Cheater
Passport Bro
What Happens in Prison
Preference
Sprinkle Sprinkle
Championship Bad
Street Exodus
Street Exodus
Street Royalty
Pawns of Power
SIS
Cartel Bloodline
Get Money Girls
Skip the Games
Til Death Do Us Part

Backpage Hustle
Link in Bio
The Virgin and The Kingpin
A Gangsta's Heart
Boosters
Can't Turn a Hoe Into a Housewife
Better you Than Me
Wig Dealer: How to Start Your wig Business
Trail Ride Blues
Demure Diva
Queen of the Carnival